New York Times bestselling author Donna Alward returns to Harlequin Romance with a brand-new duet!

Marrying a Millionaire

These tycoons make a match in a million!

Best friends wedding planner Adele and photographer Harper are in the business of happily-ever-afters, yet haven't found their own!

The arrival of two brothers, tycoons Dan and Drew, in their Banff winter wonderland may be about to change all that...

Could two Rocky Mountain marriages—and a pregnancy twist!—be in the cards?

Find out in

Best Man for the Wedding Planner

Secret Millionaire for the Surrogate

Both available now!

Dear Reader,

I'm so excited to be back writing for the Harlequin Romance line. It's always been the "line of my heart" in the Harlequin family, and writing this new duet reminded me of all the wonderful things I love about these stories. Gorgeous heroes, strong heroines and being whisked away into a swirl of emotion and happily-ever-after.

There's a scene where Drew has an up-close-and-personal encounter with a bighorn sheep. You know how art imitates life? I have a picture of me in the exact same pose (with the sheep behind me on the rocks) at Stewart Canyon, only I also have a baby in a backpack. It still cracks me up when I see it. These books have taken me back to some fond memories of time spent in Banff—both the rugged outdoors and the opulent hotel settings. I hope this Marrying a Millionaire duet takes you on a bit of an escape as well, to one of the most beautiful places on earth.

As always, thank you for reading my stories—none of this happens without you.

Donna xx

Secret Millionaire for the Surrogate

Donna Alward

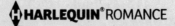

Recycling programs
for this product may
not exist in your area.

ISBN-13: 978-1-335-49919-6

Secret Millionaire for the Surrogate

First North American publication 2018

Copyright © 2018 by Donna Alward

Printed in U.S.A.

HARLEQUIN®
www.Harlequin.com

Donna Alward lives on Canada's east coast with her family, which includes her husband, a couple of kids, a senior dog and two crazy cats. Her heartwarming stories of love, hope and homecoming have been translated into several languages, hit bestseller lists and won awards, but her favorite thing is hearing from readers! When she's not writing she enjoys reading (of course!), knitting, gardening, cooking... and she is a *Masterpiece Theatre* addict. You can visit her on the web at donnaalward.com and join her mailing list at donnaalward.com/newsletter.

Books by Donna Alward

Harlequin Romance

Marrying a Millionaire

Best Man for the Wedding Planner

Holiday Miracles

Sleigh Ride with the Rancher

Cadence Creek Cowboys

The Last Real Cowboy
The Rebel Rancher
Little Cowgirl on His Doorstep
A Cowboy to Come Home To
A Cadence Creek Christmas

Heart to Heart

Hired: The Italian's Bride

How a Cowboy Stole Her Heart

Visit the Author Profile page
at Harlequin.com for more titles.

For Barb—my soul sister.

**Praise for
Donna Alward**

"This is Donna Alward at her best.... Her stories
are homey and comfy and gentle—this one is
no different."

—*Goodreads* on *A Cowboy to Come Home To*

CHAPTER ONE

March

IT WAS ODD being the person in front of the camera rather than behind it.

Harper McBride smiled once more as she looked around the room, trying to keep her smile genuine, but not quite liking the feeling of being so conspicuous. She was used to being the wedding photographer, in the background and out of the spotlight. Not tonight. The silky dress clung to her curves… what she had of them. She'd always had more of an athletic-type figure and broad shoulders that made buying tops and dresses slightly problematic. The cut of this dress, though…well, it left her shoulders bare, and a slit up the leg to midthigh left her feeling adventurous but also a little awkward.

But it was Adele's wedding day, and Harper was the only bridesmaid, and she'd do anything for her best friend.

Anything. As she'd just proved when she gave Adele and Dan their wedding present. If Harper could help her best friend start the family she'd always wanted, she was all in.

She snagged a glass of champagne from the tray of a passing waiter and took a deep drink. She only had to get through maybe another hour of the dance and she could sneak away, back to her little bungalow and into a pair of soft flannel pajamas. That was how she preferred to spend her evenings, if she wasn't photographing a wedding or special event. Out of the spotlight.

"You disappeared for a while."

A deep voice sounded by her shoulder and she suppressed a delicious shiver. Drew, the groom's brother and the best man. Harper and Drew had walked down the aisle together…and back up again when the I dos had been said, her fingers on his sleeve. Not too tightly, but not too loose, just enough to feel the warmth and strength beneath her fingertips. They'd sat next to each other at dinner, where she'd inhaled his cologne and his warm laugh had washed over her, making her smile even when she didn't quite want to. Drew Brimicombe was sexy and charming—the kind of man she didn't quite trust.

Drew and Dan were similar but also so very different. Accountant Dan kept his hair short and tidy and looked very James Bond in his tuxedo. Outdoorsman Drew, on the other hand, was a few inches shorter, his hair was a few inches longer, and he always seemed to have a little bit of scruff on his jaw. His tux fit perfectly, but there was a roughness to his appearance that was appealing. He wore designer threads as effortlessly as he wore faded jeans and a Henley shirt. Like the ones he'd worn to the rehearsal last night, and her mouth had gone dry just looking at him.

She half turned and smiled at him, her stomach flipping a little. "I went to talk to Dan and Adele on the terrace."

"It's cold outside."

"I wasn't out there very long." She lifted her glass again, hoping she wasn't blushing in the dim lighting. A small band played in the corner, some sort of jazzy blues-type music that made her think of Diana Krall. Drew's hand touched the hollow of her back lightly, and she was ready to move away when she realized he was merely guiding her slightly to the right to make room for a server with a tray of hors d'oeuvres.

His body was too close.

Just when she was ready to say something, he stepped back. "Sorry about that. She was trying to get through and I could envision a tray of cocktail shrimp going everywhere." He smiled at her, a genuinely friendly smile, but with that edge of ever-present impishness she had to guard against.

"We wouldn't want that," she replied, trying to let out a breath and calm down. For heaven's sake, he was just a guy, and she wasn't truly interested, even if he did fluster her with his sideways smile and twinkly brown eyes. After the wedding he'd be going back to California or wherever it was he called home.

"Hey, Harper?"

"Hmm?" She had been trying to keep her gaze on the band, but when he said her name, she turned back to him and met his eyes. They weren't so twinkly now, but warm and melty. At least that was how they made her feel...

"If I didn't tell you already today, you look killer in that dress."

Heat rushed into her cheeks and she bit back a curse. "Thanks. I clean up once in a while. Even break out the high heels." She tried a nonchalant shrug. "I'm more of a jeans and hoodie person."

"Me, too. But it's nice to get dressed up now and again. Especially for an important occasion like this."

She smiled. "You're right."

"I know." His confidence was at once attractive and maddening, and she snorted a laugh despite herself. When she lifted her head, he was holding out his hand. "Care to?"

He was asking her to dance. Her laughter died a quick death. She was no good at flirting, but even worse when it came to personal space and touching. She never quite knew where to put her hands or where to look. There was a reason why she spent her time behind the camera rather than in front of it. She did a good job faking it most of the time, but inside she was awkward as anything. Always had been.

"I don't really dance." She suspected that she had two left feet when it came down to it, though it had been ages since she'd tested that theory.

"I don't believe you. Besides, I think it's tradition for the best man to dance with the maid of honour."

She raised an eyebrow. "I'm letting you off the hook."

He still held out his hand. "What if I don't want to be off the hook? What are you so afraid of? I promise I'm well behaved."

She couldn't see a polite way out of it, so she put her hand in his.

He closed his fingers over hers.

Oh, no.

The butterflies in her stomach multiplied as he led her to the parquet and folded her into his arms. His scent wrapped around them, cocooning her in a cloud of masculinity. She took a breath and let it out slowly as their feet began to move.

"This isn't so bad, is it?" Piano and soft vocals swirled around them, lulling her closer to his chest. When she realized it, she shifted back a bit, putting more space between them.

"It's okay," she replied, secretly thinking it was the most wonderful thing to happen to her in months. The last time she'd been this breathless she'd been hiking near Emerald Lake and had caught a shot of a grizzly mom and cubs in the morning mist. It was one of her favorite shots, and she'd framed it and highlighted it in her studio window just off Banff Avenue.

His chest rose and fell as he silently chuckled. "Harper, you are not an easy woman."

She looked up at him, lifting her chin. "I surely hope not."

"I like challenges."

"I'm not a challenge, Drew. And not a trophy."

His eyes lit with a new light. "Thank God. I mean... I like someone who can keep me on my toes."

He tried a small turn and she stumbled a little. His arm tightened around her waist, keeping her upright.

"Careful, or I'll actually be *on* your toes," she warned.

He laughed, once again a warm sound that lulled her closer and made her smile. Damn him. Dan was a great guy, but his brother was all charm. Stupid thing was, Harper figured it was actually genuine, not an act or a cover-up. He was warm and funny and put people at ease.

At least she would be at ease if she weren't so aware of him.

"You're something else, you know that?" he said, softer now, his body brushing hers. Their feet had slowed and their steps shortened, so they were barely more than swaying. Harper swallowed against the nervous lump in her throat. She was so not confident when it came to men. Particularly good-looking ones who said all the right things without trying. They had a habit of turning around and walking away, just when you thought it was safe to believe. To trust.

"Um, thank you?" she murmured, knowing she should pull away, but wanting deep down to enjoy the moment a bit longer.

"I mean it." He leaned back and met her gaze. "Dan told me about how you've been such a good friend to Adele and all the things you did to help with the wedding. I went to your studio the other day, you know. You do some amazing work."

Heat flushed her chest and up her neck. "Oh. I... well. I didn't expect you to say that."

"Your nature photographs are some of the best I've seen. The one of the mama grizzly and her cubs? I love it."

Since it was one of her favorites, too, she smiled, more relaxed now. Talking about her work was much easier than anything overly personal. "I'm pretty proud of that one," she admitted.

"I don't know why you do weddings and stuff, not when you have such a talent for nature photography."

She shrugged. "Weddings are fun, too, you know. There's so much happiness and hope. Besides, weddings and other occasions are my bread and butter. Those bookings keep me in the black so I can indulge in the other stuff. Rent in this town isn't cheap." At least there was happiness and hope for other people. Harper just wasn't sure it was in the cards for *her*.

He nodded. "There. You're more relaxed. I'm not going to bite, you know."

She let out a breath, prepared to laugh a bit, until he added, "Unless you want me to."

The breath whooshed out of her lungs and her feet stopped moving. "Uh. Drew, I…"

"I like you, Harper. A lot."

"You barely know me."

"I'd like to fix that."

Oh God Oh God Oh God.

She decided to be honest. "I'm not good at these types of situations. I don't know what to say and I don't know how to play the game." Besides, being the loser hurt. A lot. And she was under no illusions who'd come out the victor in this match.

He tightened his fingers over hers. "Then I'll be clear." His magnetic gaze held hers. "I'm attracted to you, and I think you're attracted to me, and I'd like to know if you'd like to do something about it."

The answer in her head was *yes*, and it was so disconcerting that she stepped out of his arms as her heart started a strange gallop behind her ribs. Of course her real answer would be no. For one thing, hooking up at a wedding for a fling was not her style. And for another, she'd just offered to be a surrogate for his brother and her best friend. Talk about complicating a situation...

"I think you got the wrong idea," she said coolly. "I like you, Drew, but I'm not interested in hooking up."

He watched her for a long moment. Then his eyes warmed and he gave a little nod. "Then, I'm sorry," he said quietly, "for misreading the signals. And for making you uncomfortable."

But she was uncomfortable, and not really because of him. After all, she *was* attracted, and she'd enjoyed dancing with him and even the bit of verbal sparring they'd indulged in now and again. But it couldn't go any further, and he accepted that, so why was everything feeling so off balance now?

"Friends?" he asked, lifting a questioning eyebrow.

"Of course." She smiled and let out a breath. "It would be nice to be friends, especially if your brother is married to my bestie."

"Agreed." He held out his hand and she shook it, but when his fingers folded over hers, those darned tingles started all over again. It sucked that her body wasn't agreeing with her brain right now.

She pulled her hand away and stepped back.

Drew led her to the edge of the dance floor again, grabbed her another glass of champagne and talked to her for a few minutes about her photographs as if nothing had ever happened. Then Dan called him over, he excused himself and, with a small touch on her arm, left her alone.

Alone was what she was used to. And when she wasn't alone she had Adele, and her assistant, Juny, and phone calls with her mom and dad, who were currently living in Caicos, while her dad flew charter planes between islands. She had a good life.

But tonight, being held in Drew's arms…it had been a little taste of heaven. And one she was already regretting passing up.

CHAPTER TWO

May

HARPER HELD HER breath as she sat on the closed toilet in the tiny bathroom at her photography studio. Juny hadn't yet arrived for the day, and everything was still and quiet. Harper had wanted the few minutes of privacy to do the pregnancy test. Now she felt like she might throw up, and it had nothing to do with any potential morning sickness. It was nerves, plain and simple. A lot was riding on these three minutes of pee on a stick.

Two minutes had already passed. One more to go before she could look at the stick and know if she'd be giving her best friend, Adele, good news or bad news.

She desperately wanted it to be good. And yet the idea terrified her, too. Being a surrogate for Adele and her new husband, Dan, was something she'd really wanted to do. Adele had had cancer at a young age and couldn't have children of her own. It had taken eight long years for her and Dan to reconnect and commit to each other, even though they knew they might never have the family they both yearned for. Harper had a completely healthy uterus and no relationship to speak of. There was no reason why she couldn't carry a baby for the woman who'd made such a big difference in her world. The woman who'd made her finally feel as if she had a home and some roots to put down.

But now, with the seconds ticking away, Harper was afraid. Carrying a baby was a big thing. She'd attended medical appointments with Dan and Adele, had combed through research, had sat with her feet in stirrups. There had been little that was glamorous or sentimental about the whole procedure, but it hadn't been frightening.

Until now.

Today, if the plus sign showed up on the stick, there was no going back. She either was or she wasn't. And if she was…she'd be carrying a little human in her body for the next eight and a half months. Her mouth was dry as she tried to swallow. Thank God Adele wasn't here now, waiting. Harper wasn't sure she could have taken the pressure of Adele's heart being on the line while they waited. Better to know now, get her wits about her and decide what to say. The doctor had said this was a long shot, and probably Adele and Dan's only chance at using Adele's eggs. Either way, there would be big news for her friends. Either a second chance or the end of this particular road, and moving on to plan B.

She checked her phone. The seconds ticked down from ten…

But she didn't wait. She reached for the stick and stared at the result.

It was a plus sign.

She was carrying her best friend's baby—the most precious cargo in the world.

July

Summer sun beat down on Drew Brimicombe's head. It had been cool up the mountain, where he'd spent most of the afternoon in an alpine meadow overlooking a turquoise lake. No matter where he traveled, there was something about the Canadian Rockies that beckoned to him and made him feel at home. He'd been here half a dozen times over the past five years, mostly skiing, but now it was different. His brother, Dan, was here, and he was looking forward to some bro time.

And checking out real estate. That was his true reason for the impromptu trip—a tip from a contact about a real estate opportunity. He was always looking at expansion, and this might be his chance to open an Aspen Outfitter store north of the border. He couldn't think of a better opportunity than in the heart of the Rockies. And when one store opened, he was sure others would follow, making his brand North America-wide.

The townsite of Banff was hotter than he'd expected, though, considering how it was nestled smack in the middle of the mountains. He had on his sunglasses but not the standard ball cap he usually wore, and he could feel the heat soak into his scalp. Today had been a light hike, so he'd worn jeans, a T-shirt and a pair of lovingly broken-in boots. Water, a small digital camera, and some trail mix had been in his day pack, but he'd stayed to the marked trail and not ventured into backcountry. Not today. He'd just arrived and had chosen the easy hike to blow off the dust and claustrophobia of travel. Now he'd stop in at Dan and Adele's and let them know he'd arrived before heading to his hotel.

The house was tucked into a little side street, with a simple sign boasting Hawthorne Weddings out front. Adele's business was planning weddings, and one of her clients had been a good friend of Dan's, causing them to meet again after she'd broken his heart years earlier. No one had been more shocked than Drew when Dan had announced they were getting married, but Drew had come to the wedding and it had been clear to see that they still adored each other. Enough that Dan had uprooted his life as CFO of his company and moved here to be with her. Drew shook his head as he climbed the steps to the second floor of the house where Adele and Dan lived. He couldn't imagine doing anything like that. Settling down wasn't even on his radar, let alone leaving everything he'd worked for behind. He'd watched his dad give up dreams and aspirations for marriage and family, and he'd seen the unhappiness in his eyes.

Not that Drew didn't like Adele. He did. And Dan could make his own choices and he seemed to be happy. It just wasn't for Drew. He liked his freedom far too much.

His knock was answered by Adele, whose face lit up when she saw him. "Drew! What on earth are you doing here?"

He grinned. "Surprise trip. Are you surprised?"

"Very." But she smiled back at him. "Dan's going to flip. He was just talking about you last night. Come on in where it's air conditioned and I'll get you something to drink."

He stepped inside and heard another female voice. "Who is it, Del?"

He remembered that voice, sweet and musical. Harper. The maid of honour at the wedding. He'd turned on the charm a little, but she'd made it clear that she wasn't the type for a casual fling so he'd behaved himself.

"A surprise guest," Adele answered as Drew took off his boots. He went into the living room area in his sock feet and saw Harper seated in a plush chair, legs folded beneath her yoga-style, her hair pulled up in a pert ponytail. It highlighted her face and the light smattering of freckles across the bridge of her nose. Beautiful, he thought, but with a definite girl-next-door vibe. He much preferred her natural looks to a lot of makeup and just the right clothes. And shoes. Why women put so much emphasis on shoes, he could never figure out.

"Harper," he said warmly, stepping forward and holding out his hand. "Good to see you again."

She looked surprised at the handshake but put her hand into his anyway. "You, too." She blinked and met his eyes. "They didn't know you were coming?"

He laughed, then pulled his hand away from her soft, cool fingers. "I didn't even know I was coming. I decided yesterday to take some time off and visit, but I didn't want to call unless it didn't work out on short notice." He wasn't sure how much he wanted to say about a possible land deal. For now it was a bit hush-hush. Besides, he didn't want it to seem like he was bragging—that wasn't his style. So he left it and merely shrugged.

"Oh."

He got the sense she didn't quite approve of his spur-of-the-moment plans, so he added, "I booked a room at the Cascade. No need for Adele and Dan to be inconvenienced by my impulses."

"The Cascade, in high season? How'd you manage to get a room?" Her eyebrows shot up.

He laughed. "I lucked out. There was a cancellation."

Her face relaxed a bit and Adele came back from

the kitchen with a couple of beers and a glass of lemonade, which she gave to Harper.

"You don't like beer?" he asked, taking the bottle from Adele and twisting off the cap. "Nothing like it on a scorcher of a day like today."

Her gaze flicked to Adele and then back. "Um, I don't really drink," she answered, then hid behind her glass as she sipped. "Besides, lemonade is perfect."

He took a seat and chatted to Adele for a few minutes, catching up, but in the back of his brain he remembered the wedding and the fact that Harper had indulged in more than one glass of champagne.

Something felt off.

"So what brings you to Banff? It can't only be a visit with Dan."

He smiled at his new sister-in-law, thinking of a way to divert the conversation. "To see you, too, you know. You're a package deal now. How are the newlyweds?"

Adele's smile was huge, and her gaze flicked to Harper for a moment before shifting back to him. "Oh, we're wonderful. Dan likes his new job a lot, and I'm…" Her smile was radiant. "Well, I'm blissfully happy."

"I'm glad."

"You didn't answer my question, though. What else brings you here?"

He considered for a moment and decided to be

honest but downplay his interest. "I'm thinking about opening a store up here, and doing a little recon."

"And you can spend some time with your brother at the same time," Harper added softly.

He met her gaze, felt the jolt right to his toes. She was so pretty. So…artless. At the wedding weekend he'd learned she was a photographer. He remembered seeing her photos and realizing they were as simple and stunning as she was.

"Family's important," he said simply. "I haven't seen mine as much as I might have wanted to over the past few years."

"Dan says you two have always been close."

Harper had been smiling at him, but he dragged his gaze away to look at Adele again. "I'm the baby of the family, but I was the first to leave the Brimicombe family fold. I'd like to be around more, you know?" And look for opportunities. He was always keeping his eyes open. Being sharp was what kept him at the top of his game.

He turned his gaze to Harper. "What about you, Harper? Do you have any brothers or sisters?" Their wedding banter hadn't covered much in the way of personal subjects.

She smiled a little and shook her head. "An only child, I'm afraid. My parents live in Caicos."

"Caicos? Wow. What's in Caicos?"

She grinned. "An air charter service. My dad's a pilot."

"It's a beautiful island."

"You've been?"

He nodded. He'd traveled extensively and didn't have any plans of stopping. Stay in one place too long and he got itchy feet. Luckily, Aspen Outfitters had done well and he could indulge his wanderlust.

Adele's cell rang and she excused herself, leaving Drew and Harper alone. He looked over at her and wondered what was different. Granted, at the wedding she'd been dressed in lovely clothes with her hair and makeup done to perfection, understated but incredibly lovely. Now she was in shorts and a T-shirt with her hair in a simple reddish-brown tail. It was more than what she was wearing, though. There was something about her that drew him in and her skin glowed like she was lit from the inside. And it wasn't the summer heat. The air-conditioning made sure of that.

"You look good," he said, then realized how awful that must sound. "I mean, well."

She laughed a little. "Thanks. I think. I've been busy, but trying to take a little time off for me. It's wedding season, though. I'm booked every weekend from now until Thanksgiving."

"No summer vacations for you then, huh."

"Not really. Weddings really take up an entire

weekend, with the rehearsal on the Friday and sometimes a family event on the day following the ceremony. And sometimes couples want engagement pictures, or have an engagement party, bridal shower…"

"They hire photographers for that?"

She waggled her delicate brows a little. "If there's money? Oh, yeah."

"Do you only do weddings?"

She unfolded her legs. "No. I mean, I do things like special occasions, engagement parties, graduations, anniversaries, that sort of thing. I even had a few gigs as prom photographer for a few different schools."

He leaned forward and rested his elbows on his knees. "It doesn't leave a lot of time for your nature stuff, does it?"

She shook her head, the tips of her ponytail touching her shoulders. "Not as much as I'd like. I try to get out of the studio a few times a week and take landscapes and candids."

"Like your mama and cubs photo."

She smiled then, a genuine, happy smile that lit up her eyes. "You remember that piece."

"Of course I do. How you got such clarity with the sun coming up and the little bit of mist on the grass… I don't know how you did it."

She took a sip of her lemonade, then nodded. "The scenery here is so beautiful, and I like experimenting with different filters and lenses. I sell some of my prints, but it's not enough to make a living and pay the rent on the studio. Weddings help me keep the lights on. But that means I don't have as much time as I'd like to explore the other stuff."

Her eyes lit up when she talked about her work. He could relate. There was nothing he enjoyed more than setting up a new store from the ground up. "But as you said, weddings are on weekends. Surely you have time during the week? More than a day or two?"

She laughed, a sound as light as sunbeams. "You mean when I'm not looking after the business side of things, and editing photos? You wouldn't believe how long editing takes."

"I never thought of that."

She smiled. "I try to get out as much as I can, but lately I…"

Her words trailed off and her eyes widened, as if she'd been caught saying something she shouldn't.

"Lately what?"

Her cheeks flushed. "Oh, it's nothing. So you're looking at opening a new store. That sounds exciting."

It was a deliberate evasion and he knew it, but he wasn't going to push for information she didn't want to give. She was a relative stranger, after all, and Adele's best friend. There was no need to be rude or prying. Though he couldn't help but wonder if her glow and now her evasion had anything to do with a new relationship. It shouldn't matter, because she'd already made her feelings clear. But it did. What kind of man could capture the heart of a woman like her? He'd have to be someone special. Drew had definitely gotten the impression that Harper wasn't the type to settle for just anyone.

"It is," he replied, taking a sip of his beer. "Aspen Outfitters would fit in well here, I think, with tourists and locals alike. It's a good market. Besides, I love building a new store. I like the challenge." It certainly beat sitting behind a desk or in a boardroom. With growth came responsibility. He accepted it, but sometimes it weighed a bit heavily.

Adele came back in, bringing a bowl of pita chips and a dish of dip. She put them down on the coffee table. "I'm assuming you're staying for dinner, but I thought you might like a snack for now."

"God, your homemade hummus is to die for," Harper said, leaning forward to grab a chip and scoop it through the smooth dip.

"I laid off the garlic, too. I know it's…"

She didn't finish her sentence.

Drew helped himself. Harper was right. The hummus was delicious, and he wasn't a huge fan normally. "You don't like garlic?" he asked, before popping another chip in his mouth.

"Oh, I like it. It just doesn't like me right now."

He frowned a little. Why would there be a

change? Not that it was a big deal. It was hummus, for Pete's sake. But that was the second time one of them had stopped midsentence. He wondered if he'd interrupted something important. Something that was none of his business. He considered leaving, but then knew it would look odd if he left without at least seeing his brother.

They made small talk for a little while, until the door opened and closed again and Dan called out hello.

"We're in here!" Adele called back.

"We?"

Dan stepped into the room and Drew grinned at the look of sheer surprise on his face. He got up and gave his brother a bear hug and received one in return.

Dan clapped him on the back. "What the hell?" He laughed, stepping back. "We weren't expecting you!"

"I know. And I don't have any desire to disturb the newlyweds' love nest. I'm at a hotel."

"Don't be silly. Of course you can stay here."

Drew laughed. "Yeah, well, thanks, but I'm comfortable where I am. You guys deserve your privacy."

That Dan didn't argue further, and Adele blushed a little, told Drew all he needed to know. The hotel had definitely been the right—and most considerate—choice.

"You're staying for dinner, though, right?"

"Sure."

Dan finally noticed Harper. "Oh, and of course you're staying, too, right?"

"Oh." She looked surprised and slightly uncomfortable. "I should probably get back."

"To what? The workday's over. Stay," Adele insisted. "I'm going to grill some chicken and make risotto. I've got falafel I can make for you, unless you want something else."

Right. Drew remembered now from sitting next to her at the wedding. Harper was vegetarian.

"No, no, whatever you have is fine. You know I love falafel. Particularly if you have tzatziki from the market."

"It's settled, then."

"Let me help you in the kitchen," Harper offered, getting up from her chair. When she did, she pressed her hand to her back and stretched.

Once they were gone, Dan undid his tie and took it off, stuffing it in his pocket. He sank into a chair and sighed, then grinned. "It's good to see you, Drew."

"You, too. You guys look really happy. I'm glad."

"We are. Very."

Adele snuck in and handed Dan a cold beer, kissed his head and took off again.

"Did you really just come for a visit? It's unusual for you."

Drew shook his head. "As much as I'd be brother of the year if I said yes, I do have another agenda. Our last few stores are up and running smoothly, and I'm looking at expansion locations again. I got a tip about a property here. But I'm not saying much about it. I'm scouting things out." Of the family, Dan was the only one who knew how successful Drew had become. And they'd talked about keeping it under the radar, even with the family. Drew preferred to keep his life private, particularly his bank balance. Enough people treated him differently. He didn't need it from his family, too.

"You're looking at setting up a store here." Dan's grin was wide. "Cool."

"It's a prime location. I'm here to check out the local competition and see the property. Maybe some other locations if it's not what I'm looking for." He smiled. "And the fact that you're here is a major bonus. We haven't seen each other enough over the last five years."

Dan took a long pull of his beer. "You could have stayed here. I mean it."

"And disturb the newlywed love nest? No thanks. It's as much for my sake as it is for yours." He chuckled and took a drink of his beer, as well. "By the way, is Harper here a lot? I was surprised to find her here when I arrived."

Dan got a strange look on his face. "Oh, she's around quite a bit I suppose."

Drew put down his beer. That made at least four odd looks and a couple of halted conversations. Something was definitely off.

"Okay, I might be totally crazy, but is there something going on? You looked funny just now, and a couple of times Adele and Harper stopped midsentence. Am I missing something?" He frowned. "And if it's none of my business, say so."

Dan hesitated. "Well…it's not that it's none of your business, it's that we haven't said anything to anyone yet."

"About what?"

Dan took a drink of his beer. "Well, you know that Delly can't have kids."

"Y-es," he replied, drawing the word out a bit.

"So when I asked her to marry me, we talked about possibilities. Maybe adoption. Maybe not having children at all, which would have been fine. But at the wedding, Harper told us that she wanted to offer to be a surrogate for us."

Drew's gaze snapped to the kitchen door. He could hear Adele and Harper talking. A surrogate? He'd heard of such a thing but had never met anyone who'd actually done it. "So you're going to do it? But…how? I mean… I'm assuming you're…you know, and are you using her…" He started to stammer. "Okay, so this is actually really awkward."

Dan chuckled. "I know. It was for me at first, too. Adele had some testing done and we decided to try using her eggs. Normally this can be a bit of a long road, but we lucked out on the first try." His smile widened.

Drew stared for a minute as what his brother had just said sank in. *We lucked out on the first try.* "Does that mean… God, Dan, are you saying you're going to be a father?"

He nodded. "And Delly's going to be a mom, and Harper is carrying our baby for us."

Drew flopped back against the cushion of the chair. "Holy mackerel. I did not see that coming. That was fast."

"We haven't told anyone yet, not even Mom and Dad. She's still in the first trimester, and we want to be sure everything is okay. But since you're here…" He leaned forward, resting his hands on his knees. "I've been dying to tell someone, you know?" His grin broadened.

It made sense now. The whole garlic-doesn't-agree-with-me thing and the strange looks and truncated sentences. Drew rubbed a hand over his face and wondered what kind of woman offered to carry a child for a friend. What a huge commitment. What a generous thing. He hadn't realized that Harper and Adele were so close. What the heck was she getting out of it? He didn't consider himself a cynic, but he'd done enough business to know that hardly anyone did anything 100 percent altruistically.

"You okay, bro?" Dan lifted an eyebrow. "You look a little freaked out."

"I'm just surprised. You've only been married since March."

"We didn't want to wait. If it didn't work, we knew it could take time to adopt. I'm telling you, Harper is one in a million. Adele has gone to every appointment so far and soon we get to hear the heartbeat. That's our baby in there, you see? Adele's and mine. We'll never be able to repay Harper for this."

Harper stepped into the living room, her face easy and unconcerned. "Does anyone want another drink?"

Drew got to his feet, his emotions in a bit of a storm as he tried to adjust to the news without being an awkward ass. "Uh, I can get it. You don't need to wait on me."

She smiled softly. "Suit yourself, then. Beer's in the fridge."

He glanced quickly at her abdomen, then back up, his face heating. Harper didn't seem to notice anything and, with a flip of her ponytail, was gone back to the kitchen again.

His brain was a muddle, but he did manage to have one coherent thought as he followed her into the kitchen.

Harper is carrying my brother's baby.

CHAPTER THREE

HARPER KEPT HER hands busy cutting vegetables so she wouldn't have to look up at Drew, who'd come into the kitchen to grab a beer from the fridge. She'd seen the way his gaze had dropped to her belly and back up and the way he'd stood when she came into the room. Dan had told him; she was relatively sure of that. And it was awkward as hell.

She knew there would be some odd looks from people over the next few months, and probably more than her fair share of intrusive questions. She was prepared for that, or at least she was trying to be.

But she hadn't been prepared for Drew.

At the wedding in March he'd been crazy attractive, all sexy smiles and sparkling eyes, but she hadn't been in the mood for a wedding fling, particularly with the groom's brother. It would have been all kinds of messy.

Today had been far more awkward because the moment he'd stepped in the room her body had reacted just the same way as it had when he'd pulled her close on the dance floor. Her breath had caught and she'd felt that ridiculous butterfly feeling in the pit of her stomach. Forget the tux; Drew Brimicombe in faded, dusty jeans and a well-worn T-shirt was delectable. Add in that rough stubble and the slightly curling tips of his sun-streaked hair and she was a goner.

And she remembered how he'd propositioned her.

Now she was pregnant with his brother and sister-in-law's child and…yeah. Just as she'd thought at the wedding. This would be potentially awkward as heck and his reaction proved it. Not to mention that her attraction to him hadn't exactly disappeared.

She should never have agreed to stay for dinner.

"Harper. That might be enough cucumber."

The plate in front of her was rounded with cucumber slices and she realized she'd sliced the whole thing. To cover her embarrassment at getting caught daydreaming, she grinned and popped one in her mouth. "I can't get enough these days," she admitted. "They're so cool and fresh."

"Well, maybe you could cut some carrot and tomato to go with it?"

"Of course. Sorry. I don't know where my mind went."

Except she knew exactly where it went. With Drew, back into the living room. Or more precisely, back on the dance floor at the Cascade, being held in his strong arms, their bodies brushing.

She was peeling a carrot when she chanced a look up at Adele, who was ladling broth into the risotto. "I think Dan told Drew about the baby," she said.

Adele stopped stirring and stared at her. "You do? Why?"

"The way Drew looked at me when I went back in the room. It was the same look I got from Dan the moment I told you guys I was pregnant."

Adele frowned. "We weren't going to say anything to anyone yet. Not until after..." Adele let the thought trail away, and Harper put down the carrot peeler and went to her side.

"I know you're worried, but we're almost at the end of the first trimester. Besides, he didn't take out a billboard or anything. It's his brother. Who's here in person. Don't be too upset."

Adele let out a breath. "I know. And I don't mean to put extra pressure on you."

"I know that." Harper smiled easily, though deep down she felt as if a whole family's hopes were pinned on her keeping this baby healthy. She didn't want to be responsible for any big disappointments. "You'll feel better when you can hear the heartbeat. It's not long now. Besides, I feel great." Most of the time, anyway. Beyond a bit of fatigue and a few hours in the morning where morning sickness had become an issue.

Adele smiled and nodded. "You're right. Let's finish this up and get dinner on the table. We can eat out on the deck."

Harper finished preparing the vegetable platter, then checked on the chicken and the falafel on the grill. Adele brought out dishes for four and Harper set them out as Adele put the risotto in a bowl and brought out a pitcher of ice water.

The guys came a few moments later, still talking and laughing, and the early evening was more mellow in its heat, providing an easy warmth. Harper poured water in everyone's glass as Adele took the food off the grill, and in moments they were all seated and ready to eat.

Plates were filled, but then Drew lifted his glass. "Adele, I know Dan was supposed to keep it a secret, but I'm over the moon about your happy news." He turned his gaze on Harper, his dark eyes warm. "And you, Harper. What an incredible gift you're giving my brother and sister-in-law. To your happy family," he finished, and they all clinked glasses before drinking.

Harper looked up at him over the rim of her glass. He was watching her steadily, and those pesky nerves started again.

She was pregnant, for God's sake. One of the reasons she'd been so willing to do this now was because she wasn't involved with anyone. And it wasn't like she was thinking about starting something with Drew. He was the baby's uncle, after all. It was just that every time he looked at her she got this silly feeling all over. All she could think of was the cheeky look on his face when he'd said, *"I don't bite. Unless you want me to."*

She looked away and instead cut into her falafel.

Dinner conversation moved on to small talk about work and the summer weather, and the mood was easy and relaxed. Harper had been hungry, and the rice and falafel took away the gnawing sensation that had been bordering on queasy. When Adele asked if anyone wanted tea, the men refused but Harper was more than ready for a cup. "I'll get it, Adele. I know where everything is."

She rose from her seat and tried to ignore Drew's gaze following her as she went to the kitchen. For heaven's sake, she didn't look any different. But his perception of her had changed. That much was clear.

The kettle was on heating and she was reaching for a couple of mugs when Adele came through the sliding doors. "The boys are talking shop," she remarked, selecting a tea flavor from the selection she kept in a box on the counter. "For all Drew's outdoorsman ways, he's a good businessman. When they started talking US versus Canadian tax law implications, I had to bail."

Harper laughed lightly. "It was nice, what he

said earlier." She grabbed a mint pouch from the tea box and dropped it into her cup.

"Yeah. It's funny, though. He can't take his eyes off you."

And there went that zingy feeling through her body again. She ignored it and shrugged. "It must seem really strange." She smiled at Adele. "What we're doing is pretty unconventional."

"Are you sure that's all it is? I've known Drew awhile. I mean, we had that break where we didn't see each other at all, but when Dan and I were dating before, I got to know him pretty well. I'd say it's more interested than curious."

"I doubt it. Besides, guys don't find women who are pregnant with someone else's baby all that attractive, you know?"

"Maybe. Still. Did something happen between you two at the wedding or something?"

Harper shook her head and reached for the kettle. She poured water into the cups as she answered, the task allowing her to avoid meeting Adele's gaze. "No. I mean, we danced and stuff, but just your typical best man and maid of honour duties."

Which was an out-and-out lie.

"Well, he seems very happy with what you're doing." Adele reached over and touched Harper's hand. "As we are. We'll never be able to repay you."

Harper smiled and turned her hand over, squeezing Adele's fingers. "So you've mentioned a time or two."

"Sorry. I know I probably go on a lot."

"It's okay." Harper withdrew her hand and dipped her tea bag up and down. "I know you're excited, and I want you to be a part of this pregnancy, every step of the way. It's all good."

Except Adele had a tendency to hover a bit, and Harper wasn't sure how to deal with that. With understanding, surely. She'd rather bite off her own tongue than hurt Adele's feelings. Adele was the sister she'd never had.

They took their tea back out to the deck. The sun had dipped behind the mountains, the air cooling. Once Harper and Adele returned to the table, the discussion morphed into things to do around town, and some of their favorite outdoor activities and spots.

"Of course, Harper has to be extra careful now," Dan said, aiming a smile in her direction. "Precious cargo and everything."

Harper shrugged. "I do, but the exercise is still important. I still love going out in the mornings and getting some sunrise pictures. I can do some cool things with the lighting."

"Surely you don't go alone, though," Adele offered, sipping her tea. "I mean, anything could happen. The wildlife alone..."

Drew stepped in. "I'm sure Harper takes proper precautions. She's not naive, after all. She's been doing this a long time."

She appreciated the support and it annoyed her at the same time, as if he felt he had to speak for her when she could obviously speak for herself. Still, she didn't want to upset Adele and Dan. "I am careful," she replied. "And there's no reason why I can't maintain my regular schedule for months. I do intend to work right up until the date."

"Even wedding bookings?" Dan asked.

She shook her head. "No. I'll book until I hit eight months. I don't want to disappoint any brides. And once the baby is born, I'll take a few weeks off to recover and then get back to it."

Once the baby was born. It was a weird thing to think about. In reality, she was just the incubator. But there was no way she would come through this without having some emotions about it. She was going to feel the baby kick. Bring it into the world. She figured getting back to a regular schedule would be important.

"Still," Adele said quietly. "You won't take any unnecessary risks."

"Of course not." She knew the stakes. She'd willingly accepted them when she'd offered to do this. "I'll be careful, you know that."

The mood had dipped a little, so Harper drank the last of her tea and stood. "And now, I've totally overstayed my welcome. I should get home. Thanks for having me over for dinner…again."

"How are you getting home?" Drew asked.

"Oh, walking. It's not far." She laughed. "Nothing's really far in Banff, you know?"

"I'm going back to the hotel. I'll walk with you, if it's okay."

"Sure, if that's what you want." Harper's place wasn't exactly on the way to the Cascade, but it was only a small detour. She couldn't really say no, not after the nice toast he'd given. But she wondered why he'd want to. She didn't think it was to be gentlemanly. Drew might look all casual and laid-back, but Harper got the impression that everything he did had a purpose behind it.

Dan got up, too, and started gathering glasses. "Didn't you rent a car, Drew? You usually do."

"I did, but it's being delivered to the hotel tomorrow. The one I wanted wasn't available until today. Besides, it doesn't hurt me to walk." He looked over at Harper and smiled. "Not when the scenery is so beautiful."

Harper wasn't sure if he meant the town or if he was turning on the charm like he had at the wedding, so she ignored the comment and made her way to the door.

The night had cooled enough that Harper wished she'd thought to bring a sweatshirt, though her intention had never been to stay this late. Trouble was, Adele was a wonderful cook and Harper got tired of eating alone all the time. Now that she was pregnant, Dan and Adele tended to stay a bit close, but she understood. Adele was understandably living vicariously through Harper's experience.

She hadn't counted on Drew being around, though, or offering to walk her home. She put her hand on her tummy for a brief moment, wondering what he really thought about the situation. It might be a good litmus test to find out how the rest of his family would react when they found out.

She tucked her hands into her hoodie pockets and looked over at him. "So I guess you were pretty surprised by the news, huh?"

He nodded. "Yeah. I mean, I felt something was off, the way you and Adele seemed to talk in abbreviated sentences. So I came right out and asked Dan." He stopped walking and turned to face her. "This is a huge thing. I can't believe they asked it of you."

She smiled then. Was that his issue? In that case, she could set his mind at rest. "They didn't ask. I offered. Actually, I offered on the night of their wedding, not long before you and I danced. Adele is the best friend I've ever had. When I found out that she'd left Dan all those years ago because of her infertility, I knew I wanted to help. I told them that this would be my wedding present to them."

Harper herself was what her mom called a "miracle baby," having been adopted since her mom couldn't have children. Being able to help a family—particularly someone she loved—was fulfilling.

"Carrying a baby is a heck of a wedding gift," he remarked.

She started walking again and shrugged. "It's only for a few months out of my life, so why not?"

She saw him shaking his head out of the corner of her eye. "Not many people in this world are completely altruistic. But I can't seem to come up with a way that this benefits you. I mean, it can't be the money."

"No, you're right. It can't. Legally they're not allowed to pay me and since there's no fee for health coverage… I'm not making a penny off of this, Drew. I hope you didn't think I was."

His brow furrowed. "It crossed my mind for a minute or two."

"Then clearly you don't know me very well."

"I apologize," he said quietly. Then he looked over at her as their shoes made soft footfalls on the sidewalk. "I still find it hard to believe you'd go through something as life-changing as a pregnancy out of the goodness of your heart."

She laughed. "Life-changing as in the morning sickness, weight gain, swollen feet, stretch marks, and other things I have to look forward to?"

Drew's voice was soft and hesitant in the semi-darkness. "Well, wouldn't you want to go through those things for your own kid, rather than someone else's?"

"Maybe. Someday." She couldn't keep the wistful note out of her voice but hoped he didn't hear it. *Someday* certainly wasn't today and she wasn't sure it would ever be the right time. She tended to go on first dates, but not so many second or third ones, and she'd never had a real long-term relationship—not that she'd ever admitted that to anyone. She was twenty-eight years old, had had exactly two sexual partners, and wasn't confident that she'd ever have that life-partner-and-kid thing.

She had thought it—once. The attraction had been instant and had swept her off her feet. It had been a magical month of bliss on Caicos, an utter whirlwind that carried her away. Jared had pulled out a ring as they walked the beach beneath the stars, and she'd accepted, a 100 percent buy-in to the fairy tale. A week later he was gone, with nothing but a note explaining he'd gotten caught up in the moment and it had been "fun."

She'd been falling in love and he'd been enjoying falling into bed until he got bored—or scared. Didn't matter which. The end result was the same.

After that horrible pseudo-relationship, she'd vowed never to let herself get so carried away again.

She was far better off focusing on her business. So much so that she was considering using Juny

as more than an assistant in order to train her up
to take over a lot of the wedding and other photo
shoot duties. The girl had a keen eye for balance
and showed promise in creativity and innovation.

So she didn't say it out loud but knew deep down
that this wasn't altruistic. In her heart she felt it
might be her only chance to experience a pregnancy, and then when the baby was with Adele
and Dan, she could be Fun Aunt Harper who got
to run around in the mountains taking pictures of
marmots and bears and elk and all kinds of things.

"You do want kids, then."

His voice interrupted her thoughts and she realized they'd kept walking and were only a block
and a half from her house. "Oh. Well, I suppose.
If the right guy and the right time were to come
around." Standard response.

"How about you?" she asked, wanting to divert
the attention away from herself. "Do you want kids
down the road?"

He shook his head. "Uh-uh. I don't like being
tied down, you know? I've got the business and
that's enough. And I can pick up and travel when
I want. It's not that I don't like kids. I just like my
lifestyle better."

She got that. And she also understood what it
meant to move kids from place to place all the
time. Her dad had been in the air force and they'd
moved frequently when she was little. More than

anything she'd wanted to stay in one place and have the same school friends for more than two years in a row.

She rather respected Drew for owning his choice and not apologizing for it. They didn't feel the same way about children, but then, they didn't have to.

"Besides, I have nieces and nephews and apparently another on the way. My parents aren't hurting for grandkids."

Hers were. Though they never said a thing about it. She was an only child. Yet they refrained from any pressure to get married or start reproducing. Instead their conversations revolved around her studio and photography. She really appreciated that.

She paused and pointed at the little bungalow on a corner lot. "This is me."

"Cute place."

She laughed a little. "It's tiny and I can hardly turn around in my bathroom, but it's mine. I'd rather have a small spot to live and better space for my studio, so…"

"Cool." They stopped by the walkway leading to her front door and the silence grew slightly awkward.

"I should get in. Thanks for walking me home."

"No problem. I did have a question, though."

"Oh?" She turned to look at him, his dark eyes nearly black in the twilight. One thing hadn't changed about Drew. He was still delicious. There was no sense denying it. But she wouldn't have to worry about any more propositions. Not while she was pregnant. What kind of guy wanted to date a woman pregnant with another man's child?

"The next time you go out on a hike, can I come with you? I'm guessing you know some good spots off the beaten track that I don't."

She frowned a little. "You realize that when I hike, I go to a spot and then sometimes spend a crazy amount of time waiting, right? For the right light, or to get the right shot. It's not really a heavy-duty workout. You might be bored."

"That's okay."

"I'm off on Thursday morning and thinking of going to Stewart Canyon early, before the tourists go crazy. It's not off the beaten track, so to speak, but it's a nice walk with some good photo opportunities. Have you done the Bankhead trails on other visits? Bear in mind these are easy, popular trails. But they're interesting."

"I'm up for whatever. Just name the time."

"Then I can pick you up at the hotel at six."

"Perfect."

He gave a wave and started back the way they'd come, whistling lightly. No long look, no hand touch, nothing to suggest this was anything more than platonic and based on mutual interests.

So why was she feeling as if she'd gotten herself into a whole lot of trouble?

CHAPTER FOUR

THE DAY DAWNED CLEAR, but the sun wasn't quite up past the mountains when Drew stepped outside at five minutes to six. He was used to being up this early, either to work or get outdoors. There was a reason why he'd chosen to keep a condo just north of Sacramento. He loved the climate and the abundance of opportunities for outdoor activities in the Northern Californian forests and parks. Hitting the trail for a few hours before starting his workday was a common occurrence.

But he often hiked alone. Today he'd be with Harper, and she'd cautioned him that it wouldn't be high on the physical exertion scale. That was okay. He could do that on his own time. Instead, he was interested in watching her in action—taking pictures, that is. Pretty as she was, he wasn't interested in her romantically. How could he be, when she was carrying his brother's child? He liked her. Had, ever since the wedding. She challenged him somehow, even while being sweet as pie and as unassuming as a daisy nodding in a summer breeze.

He bent to retie his boot and gave a chuckle as he remembered her informing him that she wasn't a challenge or a trophy. That had been the moment, he realized. The moment he'd started to really admire her. The fact that she was also willing to put her life on hold for nine months to give Dan and Adele a baby only raised her in his estimation.

Though he expected if he asked her, she'd deny that she'd put her life on hold at all.

She pulled up in a tidy little SUV crossover, an all-wheel drive that would be handy in bad weather and rugged enough it would tolerate slight off-road situations. He opened the passenger door and slid inside. "Nice wheels."

She was looking a little paler than the last time he'd seen her, her freckles standing out on her nose and her cinnamon hair pulled back in a ponytail. "Thanks. I bought a lease-back so I could get something I could carry equipment in and that would handle some bumps and dirt roads." He'd barely buckled his seat belt when she started down the hill from the hotel.

"It's nice. A little more cozy than my pickup."

"You drive a truck?"

He chuckled. "Yeah. I spend a lot of time in the outdoors, and needed something rugged. Plus, you know, I needed enough room to pack some of that gear that I'm selling."

She made a turn and headed past a sign that said

Minnewanka Loop. "Well, I'll say this for you. You believe in your product."

He laughed. "I like to think of it as walking the walk." He looked at her again and frowned. "Are you okay? You look a little pale. We didn't have to go this early, you know."

She kept her eyes on the road. "It's only a little bit of morning sickness. I'll be fine by ten or so."

"That's four hours away." And what exactly did a "little" morning sickness mean?

"Yep." She exited off the highway and started up the left side of the loop. "I'll eat some crackers, drink some water. It will probably only last another few weeks. At least that's what the doctor and all the books say."

He shifted in his seat. He'd missed out on the "peculiarities of pregnancy" conversations with his sisters, since he'd moved away from Ontario. He had no idea how long morning sickness lasted or anything else to do with having babies besides what he'd seen on TV, and that was terrifying enough.

"We could have waited to go later."

She looked over at him briefly. "Oh, no we couldn't." She laughed a little. "In two or three hours the tourists will be out in full force, and I like playing with the early morning light. The nausea is an inconvenience more than anything, and I work through it."

He was glad, too. He wanted to spend the majority of his time today looking around town. In particular, the property that had recently been listed. He'd contacted a real estate agent and was anxious to get a look inside.

He enjoyed the scenery for a few moments, but it wasn't long until she pulled into a nearly empty parking lot. "It's a bit of a walk from here to the trailhead, but it's all easy. Another day I'll take you to my favorite alpine meadow, if you like." She smiled as she took the keys out of the ignition and hopped out of the car.

She was still pale, but it wasn't any of his concern if she thought she was good to go. She knew her body far better than he did, and he'd learned long ago not to presume anything when it came to women's strength and capabilities.

He'd worn jeans and a light windbreaker over his T-shirt. Last night he'd had a quick look at the trail thanks to a Google search and knew he'd be fine without his customary pack of water and snacks. It was less than five kilometers total, and since Harper hadn't mentioned going farther onto the other joined trails, he'd kept it to just the jacket, which he could fold and zip up if he got too warm.

Then he turned the corner by her back bumper and his jaw dropped.

"What the heck is that?"

She grinned up at him, a camera slung around

her neck and with a huge zoom lens on it. It had to stick out eight inches, probably more like twelve, and looked heavy as hell. "It's my camera. Wow. We really will be starting at the beginning."

"Ha, ha." He grinned and shook his head. "Seriously, how do you not have neck and back issues carrying that thing around?"

"I would if I did it all the time. And Banff isn't exactly hurting for spa services. I do get a massage now and again." She pulled another black padded bag out of the back and prepared to shift it onto her shoulders.

"No way. I'll carry that."

She lifted an eyebrow. "I carry my own equipment all the time."

"Sure, but seriously, I have nothing and you have a huge camera around your neck."

"Maybe I use it for counterbalance."

He snorted, then grinned. "Maybe you like making it difficult for me."

When she smiled back, his heart lifted. "I consider that a side benefit."

But she handed over the pack, with instructions to be careful because there was equipment in there. As well as her water and cracker stash.

The world was still and quiet as they made their way out of the parking lot and down a trail leading to the Stewart Canyon trailhead. There was nothing Drew liked better than crisp, fresh air and

the smell of everything green and alive. It was
far preferable to days in his office or shut up in a
boardroom. Birds chirped in the trees; jays, chick-
adees and awkward-looking magpies with their
long tails and raucous call. Occasionally Harper
stopped, looked above and around her and lifted
her camera to take a quick few shots. Warm-ups,
she called them, but he doubted she did anything
like a warm-up. Those photos were considered and
shot with purpose.

They met another couple coming out of the trail,
and they greeted them with a quiet hello. "There've
been some bear sightings lately," the man advised.
"Trail's not closed, but be on the lookout."

"Thanks," Drew replied, and frowned. He
hadn't thought of it before, but Harper went into
the mountains alone all the time. There were bears
and mountain lions to consider.

"I can see the look on your face," she said,
laughing a little. "If you're afraid, there's a can of
bear spray in the bag."

He stopped, and there was a look of surprise on
her face as he took the pack off his back, opened
it and rooted around for the spray. He hooked it
onto his belt loop and zipped up the pack again.
"Not afraid. Smart. The last thing I want to do is
turn a corner and find an ornery mama bear staring me in the face."

She lifted her camera. "It's one reason for the lens," she explained. "I don't have to get too close."

"Lead on, then," he said, but kept the bear spray on his hip. Chances were they wouldn't see anything, but he'd rather be prepared.

It didn't seem to take any time at all before they were at the bridge, a short expanse with the Cascade River beneath. The river ran downstream into Lake Minnewanka, and Harper stopped at the other end of the bridge and started setting up shots. He stayed back and watched, enjoying the concentration on her face, the way she adjusted a setting and tried again, or moved her position slightly. Her colour had returned, giving her cheeks more of a rosy glow, and he thought again how stunning she was. All lean legs and strong shoulders, creamy freckled skin and beautiful eyes that didn't require any makeup to make them brighter.

She stood, stretched her back a bit and sent him a grin so big he was dazzled by it.

She lifted the camera. "Oh, no," he began, lifting a hand, but she balanced the camera on her hand and put a finger to her lips, then looked over his shoulder. He half turned and nearly jumped when he realized a bighorn sheep was on the rock above and behind him, horns curled, face impassive.

When he turned back to face Harper, she was already snapping wildly, her face split with a smile that was pure fun.

He turned around and looked up at the sheep. "Good morning," he said. "Sorry to disturb." Then he backed away and crossed the bridge to join Harper. Maybe she wanted some pics of the sheep without him in them.

He waited quietly, and then the sheep moved on and Harper lowered the camera. "Sorry," she finally said. "I couldn't resist. All of a sudden there he was, standing right behind you, and you had no idea."

"He might have hurt me with those horns," Drew said, teasing.

"More like he wanted the crackers in the bag. Tourists aren't supposed to feed them, but they do. There are so many sheep that they wander through the parking lot all day long. People love it."

"Well, I'm glad I could entertain."

"Speaking of crackers, I could use a couple of mine."

He looked at her and his face blanked with alarm. Her pink colour was now pale and slightly greenish. He rushed to take off the pack but it was too late. She swung the camera around to her back, rushed to the bushes beside the path, and gagged.

Drew wasn't grossed out, but he did feel sympathy. He took out the crackers and a bottle of water and, when she was done, uncapped the bottle and offered her a drink. "Here. You can swish that around and then drink some."

She took the bottle and swished and spit, then held out her hand for a cracker. "Could I have four, please? Now that I've got the dry heave out of the way, I can eat something."

"And so begins my education into pregnancy," he said calmly, handing over several saltines. She bit into one and attempted to smile, but she looked embarrassed. "Don't worry about it," he assured her. "I've seen much worse from dehydration or heat stroke. Do you need to go back or do you want to keep on?"

She ate all four crackers and straightened. "We can go on. It's not that far anyway, and I want to get some pictures of the lake and beach. If we wait, the lake will fill up. It's the only lake in the park that permits motorboats."

"I'm game if you are."

They carried on through the woods, heading toward the lake. Drew admired her stubbornness, particularly since she'd barely eaten anything this morning. He'd at least had a shake and a protein bar before he left the hotel, and he was still hungry. What surprised him even more was when they reached a spot she liked, with a view of the shore, and she stopped and sat down on a large rock.

"Now we wait," she said. "Find a seat."

"Wait? For what?"

She grinned. "For whatever comes our way. Wildlife, a cloud that gives some fun shadows, eagles over the lake… I wait for opportunity, and when it comes, I try not to waste it."

He perched on a nearby stump and watched her adjust her camera settings. Her last words…he understood those. At least the part about not wasting opportunities. He didn't wait for them, though. He went after them. He wouldn't be here otherwise.

But he could be patient. For a while. So they sat in the quiet and waited.

Harper got up a few times and shifted position, snapping pics of the lake. A whisky jack squawked nearby, and she found it and adjusted her lens, stealthily moving and getting the bird from a few different angles before it flew away. She leaned against a tree for a moment, and he saw her brow wrinkle before it cleared. She lifted her camera and focused on the shore of the lake.

He couldn't see what she was taking pictures of, so he got up and moved as quietly as possible to within a few feet of her. What he saw made him catch his breath.

A solitary grizzly was at the water's edge, lumbering along the shoreline. He could see the varied shades of brown in its coat, feet damp from the water, the signature hump on its back, just behind the neck. "Wow," he said, and heard rapid shutter clicking as the bear obligingly turned its head to look over its shoulder and right at them…even though they were well over a hundred meters away, looking down.

She kept shooting as long as the bear was in view, but once it disappeared into the tall grass and trees again, she lowered the camera.

Her eyes shone at him, hitting him square in the gut. So blue, a luminescent shade that reminded him of the aquamarine earrings his mother wore. Her excited energy filled the air around him, making him far more aware of her than he was comfortable with.

"Did you see that? He turned around and looked right at the camera. I got some amazing shots! I can't wait to get back and look at them."

"It was incredible. You're incredible."

The words were out before he could think better of them. Her cheeks flared as she blushed and her lips dropped open a little. He found himself staring at them, wondering how they'd taste. Thankfully, the moment passed and he distracted himself by slipping the pack off his back and reaching for the water bottle. "You should have a drink before we head back. I'm assuming that we're not going farther, considering that there are bears in the area."

With perfect timing, they heard an approaching group courtesy of the "bear bells" they carried, the tinkling echoing thinly through the trees.

"Thanks," she said, taking the bottle from his hand. She kept her eyes from meeting his as she took the bottle, but she took a healthy drink and recapped it. "There's another bottle in there if you want some."

"I'm fine." He was still unsettled by the moment they'd shared. Sure, he'd been attracted to her at the wedding. But now...she was off-limits. Besides, Harper was the most dangerous kind of woman—one who could sneak past his defenses. She was extraordinary in a most understated, natural way, and if he wasn't careful he'd end up taking a wrong step.

They were quieter on the walk back, a new tension between them that hadn't been there before. Perhaps this hadn't been the greatest idea, even if he had enjoyed the few hours and watching her in action.

Tourists clogged the trail now, too, chatting and snapping pictures while posing in front of trees or the bridge, with the view up the canyon. The sheep from earlier was nowhere to be found, but they discovered several more on their way back to the parking lot, just as Harper had warned. As fun as it all seemed, Drew was glad that they'd gone as early as they had and avoided all the crowds.

She laughed as they neared her car, and he guessed it was because of the look on his face. "You were right," he said, giving a small smile. "This place gets crazy, doesn't it?"

She nodded as she took the camera from around

her neck and popped the tailgate. "This place and Johnston Canyon are really popular, but at least here the trail's a little wider. I really was planning a shorter outing today because I have a bunch of editing to do the rest of the day. But later, maybe early next week, I'm going to head up to Healy Pass and make a whole day of it. It's about sixteen kilometers or so round-trip."

But she didn't invite him along, and he didn't ask. First of all, he probably wouldn't be here next week. And second, it wouldn't do to spend too much time with her. Before he knew it he'd lose his perspective and start something he had no right to start. It was better if they went their separate ways.

He got in the car and put on his seat belt. Instead of going back the way they came, Harper drove around the other side of the "loop," coming out by the pond and picnic area where a few cars of tourists stopped and took pictures of the elk wandering nearby.

"It wouldn't be Banff without elk being everywhere," Harper said, smiling a bit. "You never know where they're going to pop up, either in town or in the fields or roadsides."

"It's like they're part of the scenery," Drew said. "Tell me, do you like tourist season? The town seems awfully crowded."

"It's a resort town, so that's what's expected. But you know, there are places around town that aren't part of the bus tour stops and day trips. There are a few places that are more popular with townies than tourists. And honestly, I mingle with some of the other business owners near the studio. I have my assistant, Juny, who's young and energetic and fun. I have Adele, and now Dan. So no, I don't mind tourist season. It's what keeps me in business, and the studio and shop do better business in the summer." She turned back onto the highway and looked over at him. "Pictures like today? This canyon is a recognizable landmark. If any are worth blowing up, I'll showcase them and sell them to tourists who want to take home a little reminder of where they were."

"And the other shots?"

She grinned. "If any of those bear shots are worthy, I'll mat and frame a couple."

"Like your mama and cubs."

"Which still hasn't sold, but it's good enough I'm not going to give it away."

Good, he thought. As a businessman, he often saw people charging too little for their goods rather than commanding a price that was proportionate with the quality.

She dropped him back off at the Cascade, pulling up beneath the overhang at the lobby doors. "What's on the agenda for the rest of your day?" she asked.

"Heading into town to look into a few businesses." He deliberately kept his wording vague. Other than Dan, no one knew he was looking at a major acquisition, and that was how he wanted it. "I'm going to spend a few days doing that, actually. Maybe there won't be room for another outfitter here, you know?"

"And then?"

He shrugged, his hand on the door handle. "I don't know. There are lots of places in British Columbia I can consider. And northern Alberta…lots of good fishing up there."

He couldn't read her expression, but she didn't look overly impressed. "What's wrong?"

"Is it all about moving around for you?"

"Why not? I'm young and have all kinds of energy for this sort of thing. I love traveling and moving around. And man, the challenge in setting up a new store is really exciting."

"But what about when that stops? When is it enough, and what will you do then?"

It was an odd question, he thought. And it seemed there was something more behind it than plain curiosity.

The words to tell her how successful he was were on the tip of his tongue, but he held back. If he were honest with himself, he felt more like his premillionaire self when he was with her. No expectations or trappings of success. An easy hike in the mountains. Jeans and T-shirts and a little dust on his boots. Hell, he hadn't looked at his cell phone since last night, and that was nearly unheard of.

So he kept the words back and shrugged.

"I haven't thought that far ahead. I like my life. I like the challenge and the variety and the ability to move around. I don't see that stopping anytime soon."

"I see."

"You don't sound convinced."

They were idling in the passenger drop-off, but it wasn't overly busy at the moment so he waited for her answer, removing his hand from the door handle and placing it back into his lap. The last thing Drew ever wanted was to feel trapped in one spot. Drew loved his parents, and they'd provided a good, loving home for their children. But sacrifices had been made and resentments had taken root because of it. His dad in particular had sacrificed his dream job for his family, and seeing the defeated look in his father's eyes had stuck with Drew all these years.

Harper sighed. "It's a personal thing for me is all. Travel is one thing, and I get that. Who doesn't love a vacation, going new places and seeing new things? But moving around all the time, that rootless kind of existence? I did that for most of my young life, and it was hard. Really hard. I like having some stability now, is all. But that's my life, not yours." She smiled encouragingly. "Of course you should live yours how you want."

"As should you," he replied. "I guess we're not much alike, are we?"

Her gaze touched his, and that spark sizzled between them again. "No, I guess we're kind of opposite in a lot of ways."

"Except we like the outdoors."

"Except that."

"And the fact that we both love Adele and Dan a lot."

Her eyes warmed. "That, too."

And with that he knew he had to leave. Harper had complication written all over her and as much as he was enjoying this…interlude, he knew it wouldn't last. "I'd better let you get out of here before the next tour bus lands. Thanks for taking me with you, Harper."

"You're welcome."

He got out and shut the door, then lifted a hand as she drove away.

He couldn't let himself think about her or why she'd been bounced from place to place, or how her eyes darkened to nearly sapphire when awareness flickered between them.

He was here for three or four days, tops. Surely he could avoid her for that long, couldn't he?

CHAPTER FIVE

HARPER SAT AT the computer and went over the photos from the morning. There were two that she particularly liked: one of the whisky jack sitting on a spruce branch, and one of the shots of the grizzly looking right at the camera. That had been a lucky, lucky thing and would take only a little editing to make it sing.

Then there were the ones of Drew and the bighorn sheep. She paused over those, unable to suppress a smile as she looked at the one where he'd turned and spoken to the animal, their eyes locked on each other. Then there was another where he was laughing about something and it made her heart give a strange thump. It was unfair he had to be so damned handsome and charming.

He'd been a good sport, too; patient and quiet when he needed to be. And he'd minimized her embarrassment when the nausea had gotten the best of her and she'd been sick.

He was a good guy; she knew that. But that was where it ended. It wasn't just the awkwardness of the situation. It was his whole lifestyle, traveling for work and opening new stores and not being rooted in one place. Nowhere was really…home. That kind of nomadic existence simply wasn't for her.

Home was the one thing she'd always wanted. Not that hers hadn't been full of love; it had. She couldn't have asked for better parents. But the nature of her dad's job had been one of moving from base to base, or being alone with her mom while he was deployed. It had been hard to put down roots, and instead of roots Drew had wandering feet.

Good to look at. Even talk to. Not boyfriend material. In March she hadn't been looking for a fling. She rested her hand on her still-flat stomach. She certainly wasn't looking for one now, either.

Juny came into the back room to grab her water bottle and did a double take at Drew's picture on the screen. "Oh my gosh. Who is that?"

"Dan's brother, Drew. Remember? From the wedding?" Juny had helped her go through the photos, and together they'd chosen the best ones for a portfolio for Dan and Adele.

"Sure, but he was all done up in a tux then, and his hair was shorter. He's hot."

"I didn't think that hot guys were on your radar." She grinned up at Juny, waggling her eyebrows. Juny's girlfriend, Renée, had just moved in with her in an apartment in Canmore.

"Depends on the radar. I can appreciate a fine form, no matter the gender. And Drew Brimicombe is a fine form. I like his outdoorsy look."

"Me, too," Harper replied, then realized she shouldn't have said anything. Juny got a speculative look on her face and pulled up a chair. The bell over the door would ring if someone came into the storefront. There was no way Harper was going to be able to avoid Juny's prying.

"Spill," Juny commanded, and leaned forward, ready to get the goss.

"There's nothing to spill. Like you said, I can appreciate a fine form."

"Yeah, but he's on *your* radar."

"Not really." Harper made sure she flipped through another few pictures. "I mean, he flirts but I'm not really interested. I've got other things going on."

She hesitated after that last bit. Juny didn't know about the baby, but Harper would have to tell her soon. Maybe in a few weeks, when the first trimester was officially over. It felt odd, keeping something that special a secret from the employee she liked so very much.

"Things like what? Wedding season?"

"Sure. It's busy around here, or haven't you noticed?"

Just then the bell rang, announcing a new arrival. "Saved by the bell," Juny advised drily, arching an eyebrow.

"Yeah, yeah," Harper replied, but she laughed a little.

The next few days were busy ones, and Harper spoke only once to Adele and not at all to Drew, not that she'd expected to. She'd had a wedding rehearsal and then wedding day, and on Sunday she'd been exhausted. Monday she had a doctor's appointment in Calgary.

Adele went with her and Dan met them at the office. At a little over eleven weeks pregnant, she was close to being past the first trimester, and she knew everyone would feel some relief. When the doctor put the Doppler against her tummy and moved it around, she flinched a little. Dan and Adele looked so excited and expectant. If something happened and they couldn't find a heartbeat today, they'd be so disappointed.

But it came through loud and clear. *Bu-bump bu-bump* galloped in her ears, much faster than a grown-up heartbeat. Adele started to cry. Dan held her hand. And Harper stared at the doctor, marveling that a little human was growing inside her.

For someone else.

It was right and she was glad of it, but something strange and new blossomed in her chest. Maybe this baby didn't have any of her DNA, but he or she was still a part of her even if she wasn't a part of them. She bit down on her lip and kept listening to the rhythmic sound of that tiny beating heart. She didn't want it to stop.

Dan took out his phone and hit the record button. "Today we get to hear our baby's heartbeat!" Excitement rang through his voice as he angled the camera at Adele's beaming face and then over at Harper, who felt a little self-conscious with her belly exposed.

But she smiled anyway, unable to resist the joy in the room. The tears on her best friend's cheeks told her what she needed to know. This had absolutely been the right decision.

The doctor took away the wand and Harper suddenly felt bereft. She loved the sound of that heartbeat, a quicker version of her own. It touched her in ways she had expected and yet couldn't possibly anticipate. Everything was suddenly so *real*.

In six months, she would birth this little human and put him or her in Adele's arms.

Was it wrong that she felt the need to hold them close until then? That she should feel so…attached?

"Harper, are you all right?"

"What? Oh, of course!" She put on a bright smile. "I'm so relieved everything is going well, you know?"

The doctor nodded. "It is. Everything is right on schedule. Are you still feeling sick?"

Harper nodded. "Yes, in the mornings. But it's nothing I can't handle. By midmorning I seem to come around okay."

"Okay, but if this goes on for many more weeks, come back in. We can look at some medication. Mostly we need to make sure you and the baby are getting good nutrition."

"I will," she promised. "And I'm eating well, I promise. I've been following a vegetarian prenatal diet quite closely."

The doctor looked at all of them. "Well, you're good for another month. You can make your next appointment at reception if you like. You'll get booked for an ultrasound at that appointment, as well. Have you thought about having an amnio?"

Adele looked at Harper, then at Dan. "I know using my eggs was possibly a bit risky, but I'm not sure I want to take the chance on anything going wrong. I know there are risks with the amnio, too, and I…" She reached over and took Harper's hand. "I think this whole thing is a miracle and we'll take the end result, even if that means special challenges."

Dan put his hand on her shoulder in silent support.

"Well, there's no need at the moment, and from all indications everyone seems to be doing fine. We'll chat again at the next appointment, unless something comes up between now and then."

The doctor paused to give Harper's shoulder a squeeze and then left the room.

"That was pretty amazing," Dan said, tucking his phone in his pocket.

"I know. But guys…" Harper looked up with a wry smile. "I really want to get this goop off my stomach."

Everyone laughed, and then Dan and Adele left the room to let Harper put herself back in order.

She wiped the gel off with a tissue, but before she pulled up her yoga pants again, she put her palm against her stomach. "I heard you today, little one," she whispered. "We're in this together, you hear? So you stay healthy in there. We're almost a third of the way there."

And if the backs of her eyes stung a little, she'd blink it away and be thankful. She needed to embrace this experience and not hide from it, even though she suspected that when it was all over her heart was going to be a little bit tender.

On Tuesday, Drew showed up at her studio.

"You're still here," she said, her voice friendly as she greeted him in the showroom. "I wondered if you'd headed back to parts unknown."

"Not yet. Actually, I think I've found a location. I spent most of the day yesterday on conference calls with my executive team. I'm meeting the property owner at three today to see if we can hammer out a deal."

"That was fast." She blinked and stared at him. He'd been here only a week.

"When I see something I want, I don't waste time."

She pondered that. Drew definitely didn't seem like a patient kind of guy. Not necessarily reckless, exactly. But he definitely wasn't the kind of man to sit and wait around for opportunities to come to him. Which was kind of funny, because a lot of her day-to-day existence consisted of just that. Sitting around. She'd learned patience that way, and trust. "Sometimes I think the best plans happen when you're willing to sit in the quiet and wait for them. Like the grizzly the other day."

"Ah, but you still went after it." He put his hands in the pockets of his khaki shorts. "You made a plan and put yourself in the right spot at the right time. That's preparation meeting opportunity."

She laughed. "I know theoretically you're right. I think there's a slight philosophical difference in our thinking. Anyway, that's great, as long as you're happy about it."

He seemed happy. His eyes were lit up and he had an air of confidence and satisfaction that was... well, charismatic. She'd never denied that he was attractive or that she was attracted to him. It was more about choosing not to pursue something that would be short term and not, well, meaningful. No matter how...

Her gaze fell on his lips, slightly parted, an imperfect bow shape that looked utterly kissable.

No matter how sexy he was...or how amazing it might be to be his, even for a moment.

She looked away. Ugh, she had to stop thinking like this! It had to be the hormone surge or something. She was normally far more levelheaded and less obvious. After Jared's abrupt departure from her life, she'd vowed to make sure never to let herself fall until she was sure it was exactly what she wanted. And Drew wasn't it...no matter how alluring he was.

"Did you want to see the pictures from the other day? A few turned out really great." She started to lead the way to the back room. Juny had run out for coffee, but there was no worry about leaving the storefront empty. Foot traffic was light today and the electronic bell would always ring if someone came in.

"I'd love to. Was the bear one good?"

"There were a couple from that sequence that I like a lot."

She stopped by her computer and sat; he leaned over her shoulder, close enough she could smell his spicy aftershave. She inhaled deeply, imprinting the scent on her brain. This really was going too far. Hadn't she decided that they were too different? Opposites might be exciting, but it could also cause a lot of friction.

And why was she continually trying to talk herself out of liking him?

"Wow. I love that one."

She'd pulled up the picture of the whisky jack first, letting the grey-and-white bird fill the screen. "He's pretty, isn't he?"

"Very. That's such a soft grey." He pulled up a chair and sat beside her, leaning over to peer at the monitor. "Know what other bird has a gorgeous grey colour? An albatross. Their heads are amazing. It seriously looks like a watercolour."

"I didn't think they were grey." She spun in her chair to face him, getting a jolt when she realized how close their faces were. There was a half second where he paused, the miniscule flash of time it took to take half a breath, and then he leaned back a bit, settling in his chair a bit more. Heat rushed up her neck.

"There are different species, with slightly different sizes and colourings," he said, moving back into the topic smoothly. "Look up a grey-headed albatross. I saw them on a New Zealand expedition to Macquarie Island."

Of course he had. She'd traveled some and had moved around within Canada a lot, but Drew was a different sort of traveler. He was an adventure seeker. Part of her was jealous that he'd had such trips, and totally envious of the photographic opportunities. Another part was simply curious.

"Did you see penguins?"

He laughed. "Tons. Like this ginormous rookery with thousands and thousands."

She sighed. "That must have been amazing."

"You haven't seen them?"

"Only at the zoo. And once at SeaWorld, when I was a little kid."

"Would you like to?"

She turned in her chair. "Is that an invitation?" At his surprised expression, she laughed. "Just kidding. But yeah, I'd like to. I'd like to photograph tons of different ecosystems. Right now, I'm here, so I'm focusing on my backyard. There's lots to keep me busy."

He sat back in his chair and tapped his lip. "But where would you go if you could go anywhere in the world?"

She thought about it a long time, struggling for an answer. "I've always wanted to go to Iceland. The geography is so unique and I have a secret wish to photograph an Icelandic horse." She met his gaze. "I suppose that sounds silly. But you see…no other horse is allowed on the island. They're incredibly unique and untouched."

But his warm eyes held hers. "Not at all. I wish I could take you on some armchair travel, but that's one place I haven't been, either. Though I've been to Norway."

Of course he had.

"Aspen Outfitters must be doing really well for you, if you can travel so much before you're even thirty."

"It does okay."

It was a rather bland answer, and she puzzled for a moment, but his financial status and how he spent his money wasn't any of her business.

"It keeps you in passport stamps," she said lightly.

He laughed a little. "It does. Last year I went zip-lining in Costa Rica."

Harper's eyes widened. "Zip-lining in the jungle? No thanks. I'm afraid of heights."

"Really?"

She nodded. "Really. I don't even like getting up past the second step on a stepladder."

His eyebrows lifted. "I wouldn't have guessed that. How do you manage skiing, or the gondolas? Surely you've done both, living here."

She smiled weakly, her stomach doing a little nervous flip just thinking about it. "I take deep breaths. I don't look down."

His eyes lit up. "You know, one woman in our group was terrified. She was literally crying on the platform. But she did it—took that step off, and she loved it. Couldn't wait to keep going."

Harper shuddered. "Good for her," she said drily, and then they both burst out laughing.

Now they were sitting there smiling at each other like idiots, and as the moment drew out, she wanted him to lean over and kiss her.

The doorbell sounded out front. "Excuse me for a moment," she said, scrambling to her feet. "I'll be right back."

It was Juny, who'd returned with a coffee for herself and an iced fruit-infusion tea for Harper. "I got them to add a splash of soda water for some fizz," Juny said as she handed over the cup.

Harper thanked her and told her to take the money out of petty cash and then took a deep breath, grateful for the interruption, before going back to Drew again.

"Sorry about that. It was Juny, bringing back some drinks." She took a sip of the cold tea—cranberry and pomegranate from the taste of it—and sighed. It was delicious and refreshing, just what she needed.

"No worries. But I would like to see the bear before I ask you for a favor."

A favor? Curiosity whetted, she resumed her seat and brought up the thumbnails, then picked one of her favorites.

"Oh, man," Drew said, drawing a breath. "He's huge. That's magnificent."

Her heart leaped a little at his praise. "I like the

balance of it, and the grey tones of the rocks play with the water and the coolness of the green in the evergreens."

She hesitated. "There are other ones where I'd adjusted the exposure, but I don't like them as well. Even with this one, I considered changing the hues slightly, or playing with the contrast, but I actually like it as is. I just made a few minor tweaks."

He was quiet for a moment. "You're right. The eye's drawn to the bear itself. The rich brown really stands out."

She was pleased he understood. "Now, want to see something fun?"

She scrolled until she got a photo of the canyon, the narrow expanse of water with the forest on either side. She brought up her editing software and made a few clicks. The photo changed and Drew let out a quiet, "Oh, cool."

"Right? It's fun to play with." She'd basically turned her photo into a watercolour painting. "If I change the opacity and contrast a little, the definition of water against the sky is better." She dragged her cursor and watched the shades pop a little more.

"Do you do a lot of editing this way?" he asked.

She shook her head. "Not really. I play with it, mostly. Like…look at this." She opened up a picture of a wild rose. "This is an 'underpainting' feature. What do you think?"

"I think someone could easily go down a rabbit hole of playing with all sorts of photos and wake up a week later."

She giggled. "Pretty much."

"Know how those would look great?"

She frowned. "How?"

"If you took some of your favorites and did them up as greeting cards or postcards in the storefront. You could keep the gallery as is, but add a small section near the counter for cards or smaller photos, perhaps pre-matted."

He wasn't wrong. Except...

Except it felt like commercializing on something that she took very seriously. Reducing it to a short-term consumable that could easily be tossed aside, rather than appreciated and cherished.

But what Drew saw was a business opportunity.

"It's an interesting idea," she offered, feeling the need to toss him a crumb, although she didn't know why.

"I have them now and again. And now...for my favor. Could you come with me this afternoon? I'd like for you to see the building I'm considering. Tell me if there's something I'm missing."

"Why me?"

"Because you have a sharp eye and attention to detail. I went in and saw all the possibilities. But I'd like a second pair of eyes to go through it with me this time, and pick out where I'm going to have issues."

She chuckled. "I am so flattered that you want to use me as a fault-picker."

"No, no, no. Attention to detail, remember?" But he smiled, too. "What do you say?"

"You want to go now?"

"I can have the Realtor meet us there." He hesitated. "As long as you're not too busy. I know you have your own business to run."

It would be an excuse to spend more time with him. She knew she shouldn't want to, and then wondered why the heck not. Lately her whole life had consisted of work, feeling tired and sometimes nauseated, and no social life beyond Adele and Dan, where again, the talk was always of the baby. As the days went on, she found herself getting more and more attached to the tiny life inside her. So much so that she knew she had to keep her mind on the big picture. Like other parts of her life, and what she was planning to do after the baby arrived and she went back to her normal routine.

None of which she felt she could discuss with anyone, because she had been the one to suggest the surrogacy and she didn't want to appear to be a complainer.

"I can spare an hour or so." Actually, the idea of leaving the studio and walking through town in the sunshine sounded blissful. "Where's the building?"

"Half a block off Banff Avenue, right near the Ptarmigan Inn. I looked at a few other spaces, but none had the square footage I need and the only other one that did wasn't as central."

"Sounds logical. Let me close this down and I'll be right with you."

He went back out to the storefront and she could hear him talking to Juny as she closed her programs and shut down her computer. Deep down she got the feeling she might be stepping into trouble, but she'd been doing the same things day after day for too long. This weekend she'd be at a wedding the whole time. Why not enjoy an afternoon off, particularly in the company of someone as sexy and funny as Drew?

CHAPTER SIX

DREW WAITED FOR Harper out front, and spent his time first contacting the Realtor, then chatting to Juny. She looked cute with leggings and boots and a colourful flowy top of some sort, a pair of dark brown braids touching each shoulder. But when Harper came out from the back room, his breath caught. She was wearing a simple denim skirt and a peasant blouse, little sandals on her feet, and her hair was in what he realized was a customary ponytail. He couldn't tell if she was wearing makeup or not. It didn't matter. Harper was just…different.

He shouldn't be here. She'd said as much when she'd dropped him off the other day. But he couldn't help it. A few quiet hours and the first thing he did was find himself walking toward her gallery, eager to see her teasing eyes and smiling face.

"I'm ready if you are," she stated, slinging a small bag over her shoulder.

"Should I close up?" Juny asked.

"I can come back. You don't have to stay until six."

"It's no trouble. I'm meeting some people at seven, so it works out fine."

"Then sure. Taking a few extra hours would be amazing. Thanks."

Drew held the door for her and they stepped out into the afternoon sunshine. "I parked a half block over, and we can take my ride if you want."

"You did get your rental."

"I did. It makes it easier if I have to run to showings or meetings. But we can walk if you want."

"It's a beautiful day. Let's."

The day was hot but with that crisp-mountain-air feeling. Sidewalks were swept and kept clear, with hanging baskets on the streetlamps and brightly coloured planters outside each business. He looked over at Harper, who'd slid on a pair of sunglasses against the glare. She looked good, but he missed being able to see her eyes.

"Does Juny know?" he asked.

She looked over at him. "You mean about the baby?"

"Yeah."

"Not yet. I have to tell her soon, though. Other than the doctor, you're the only one outside the three of us to know anything."

He felt oddly privileged, even though he knew it was just because he was in town. Plus it made him feel as if they shared a secret.

He heard an odd gurgle and saw her cheeks turn a bright pink. "Did you eat lunch?"

"Not yet, but I thought we had to meet your guy."

"We do. But ice cream." He pointed to the Cows Ice Cream store. "And you need your dairy, don't you? Calcium and all that?"

She laughed. "And fat, and sugar...but I love ice cream. It's one of my secret vices."

"You have more than one? I don't believe it."

Then she nudged him with her arm and he felt a warmth slide through him. He genuinely liked her so much.

"I have many. I keep them hidden."

He looked at her again, gave her an assessing up-and-down glance and shook his head. "Nope. Still don't believe you. You're too sweet."

She barked out an unladylike laugh and he couldn't help but grin from ear to ear. They were still smiling when they looked both ways and scooted across the street to the Cows Ice Cream shop.

It was summer. There was a line.

But he didn't mind. He watched as Harper scanned the flavor menu, her sunglasses now perched up on top of her head. It had been a long time since he'd enjoyed someone's company so much. She wasn't the type to expect expensive and intimate dinners and big romantic gestures. A cone of ice cream, or a walk in the forest… Harper was the kind of woman who appreciated little things.

Lately it seemed that anyone he tried to date within his business circle came with an expectation of… He frowned a little. Status? A certain standard? Whatever it was, it frequently left him feeling like they were interested in what he could provide rather than interested in *him*.

He wanted to think money hadn't changed him, that it had just made things easier. Like this trip. He could stay in a hotel for two weeks at summer rates and not worry about maxing out a credit card. It didn't mean he needed or expected five-star anything. Did he? Had he really changed over the years, as his success had grown?

He thought about his day-to-day life and realized he had lost touch with what it was like to be… well, *normal*, for lack of a better word. Sure, financially he'd found it rougher in those days, but his success came with a price, after all, as much as he downplayed it. And that could be summarized in one simple word: *responsibility*. He was responsible to his shareholders, responsible for the people who worked with and for him. As the man at the top, sometimes it was hard to know whom to trust.

His lifestyle was nice, but being with Harper reminded him of the guy he used to be and had lost a little along the way. Easygoing, laughing more, up for a cone of ice cream as a special occasion.

"I'll have a small Cowconut Cream Pie," Harper ordered, then looked back at Drew. "And what are you going to have?"

Her voice drew his attention back to the task at hand. He really didn't care, but he gave the flavors a cursory glance and replied, "Fluff 'n' Udder."

Harper giggled.

"These names are ridiculous," he said firmly, but his lips twitched. "And I like peanut butter, so hush."

They gathered their cones, Drew paid and they made their way back out into the sunshine again.

The ice cream was cold and rich and delicious, but it also melted fast so they put decorum aside and took substantial swipes with their tongues, catching it before it ran down the waffle cones. Once Harper looked over and snickered, then took her napkin and wiped a dot off his chin.

Their cones were almost gone when she took a bite of the waffle and it left her with a dollop of coconut ice cream on the spot where her upper and lower lip met.

He didn't think, didn't analyze, didn't weigh pros and cons. He simply stepped forward and kissed it off, his lips lingering on the corner of her mouth as she froze in surprise. Then she let out a soft, gentle sigh, and he closed his eyes and slid his mouth ever so slightly to the right, kissing her properly while she responded sweetly, with a hint of hesitation and shyness.

She tasted so good, which had absolutely nothing to do with the ice cream. He lifted his hand and cradled her neck a bit as he briefly deepened the kiss, sliding his tongue into her mouth, and then retreating, aware that they were in the middle of Banff Avenue and that Harper was not likely the PDA type. Neither was he, for that matter.

"Oh," she said softly, and her confused blue eyes lifted to capture his.

"I should probably apologize," he replied, his voice equally quiet. "But I don't want to. Because that was—"

"Please don't apologize," she interrupted. A weak smile curved her lips. "I liked it."

That bashful admission did more to fuel his libido than any R-rated proposition she might have whispered. He looked down and found peanut butter and chocolate ice cream dripping off his fingers. What a dangerous distraction she was turning out to be.

They dumped their cones in a nearby trash can and Harper reached inside her purse for a little pouch of glass cleaner cloths. "They're not perfect, but they should get the stickiness off. I keep them for my lenses."

They wiped their hands and then Drew reached down and twined his fingers with hers. "Are we okay? That was totally impulsive, but I don't want to assume anything."

Her cheeks coloured once more. "We're okay," she answered, giving his hand a squeeze and then sliding her fingers out of his. "It's not like I haven't thought about it." She started to walk away.

He reached out and grabbed her arm. "Since when?"

She spun around and met his gaze with laughing eyes. "Since the wedding. Just because I said no doesn't mean I didn't consider it for five seconds. Or that I haven't wondered."

She did a great impression of having a ton of self-control, but the soft pliancy of her lips and the way she'd sighed had told him plenty.

"That doesn't mean I think this is a good idea, though," she continued, and the buoyancy in his chest took a nosedive. "We're very different people. You're only here for a little while and I still don't do flings. Plus the pregnancy complicates matters."

He wasn't sure how to tell her that if anything, it made her more attractive to him. Plus she wasn't going to be pregnant forever.

"Because of Dan?"

"You don't consider it odd that we're talking about…us…" She hesitated over the word, frowning. "And that I'm carrying his child?"

A handful of tourists looked their way, and

Harper quickened her step so that he had to trot to keep up. Did she even know where she was going?

"It's not like you slept with him."

"No, of course not." She turned and faced him then, the frown deepening until there were matching creases between her brows, right above her nose. "It's still weird."

He wasn't going to argue with her, so he let the topic drop—for now. If she felt it was odd, well, her feelings were her feelings. He had no problem stepping up and taking the lead but he also knew when to back off and listen, so he did. "We need to cross the street again."

"I know."

The real estate agent was already waiting for them, and he opened the door to the building and let them walk in ahead of him.

Drew loved the space, and had from the first moment. Oddly enough, it wasn't the initial property that he'd come to see. That one had been okay, but too warehouse-feeling for his liking. This space was a bit smaller, but it had charm to spare. Wide open, with supporting wood beams, thick cross-beams in the ceiling and a second floor with a loft that overlooked the main level.

"Oh, this is lovely. And prime location. I can't imagine what this would cost you."

He tilted his head a bit and watched her move into the large center space. Not once had she mentioned his financial status, though she must know. She was best friends with Adele, after all. It was refreshing, being viewed for himself and not his net worth. If she wasn't going to bring it up, he certainly wasn't.

"The open concept would work great, don't you think?"

Her voice broke him out of his thoughts. "I do."

She stepped farther inside, went to the middle of the room and turned in a full circle. "Cash and customer service over there." She pointed. "Otherwise, if you have lines, you'll end up blocking access to the stairs. If you intend to use it for retail space, that is."

"I'd like to."

"Then you'll have to have an accessibility plan," she said quickly.

She was right. He hadn't thought of that, but he should have. "It's too good a space to waste."

"I agree."

He let her wander around for a few minutes, and could almost hear her brain turning. The Realtor was smart enough to stand back as well, and sent Drew a quiet smile.

She looked at the front windows and then back at him. "Lose the awnings in the front. It'll hide your window displays, and you want them dynamic and visible. They'd be fine for a café or something, but not Aspen Outfitters."

The Realtor nodded. "I told him the same thing."

"You're looking to buy, not rent, right?"

"That's right. When I decide on something, I go all in."

She lifted her brows. "And what if you lose?"

"I win more than I lose. And I always take calculated risks, not foolish ones."

"In other words, it doesn't happen often."

"Nope."

A smile broke over her lips. "Then why am I here again? Clearly you had your mind made up."

"Because before I leap I always want a second opinion. And you know the area. Do you think the town can handle another outfitter?"

She nodded. "It's a big business around here. Some will still shop in Calgary first, but with a good supply and competition here, you'll probably see increased traffic."

Which was his thinking, too, and he'd run some data as well—annual visitors, local populations, volume on marked trails each year or people using tour companies for backcountry expeditions. Nothing was a sure bet, but this felt good.

"And the upstairs…"

"You know what sells better than I do. You could put clothing up there if you wanted, and create a kind of boutique. But if you want to push it on the lower level, there might be some other department you want to put upstairs." She gave him a nod.

"Your people will be able to tell you that far better than I can." She smiled. "My photographer's eye likes the balanced feel of it."

The Realtor looked at Drew, who gave him a brief nod. "You have my offer. It stands."

"And your threshold?"

"No more than ten percent above the initial offer. He knows he won't get full asking price. Even for a prime location like this."

"I'll be in touch."

"Shall we?" Drew asked, sweeping his arm out to the side to invite Harper to join him in the sun again.

"That's it?"

He nodded. "Yep. That's it. Now I wait. It'll be a back-and-forth of offers and negotiations now, but I'm guessing we'll have a verbal agreement by tonight and start the ball rolling tomorrow with paperwork.

"And then what?"

He smiled. "Then it's up to the bank. I'll sign what I need to sign, start putting everything in order and then head back home and get the ball rolling on the whole new-store process." He grinned. "This'll go much faster than when we actually build a store from the ground up. A crew will go in and do the renovations, and then we can start the hiring process and shipping stock. All told…we'll probably open in January, give or take."

She was quiet beside him. "Sorry, are you okay?" he asked. "You got quiet all of a sudden." It struck him that she might not be feeling well. "Is the ice cream not settling well?"

She smiled a little and they kept walking. "Oh, I'm okay that way. The morning sickness is getting a little better. There's really only an hour or so in the morning where I feel awful, and then it goes away. I'm hoping it'll disappear altogether really soon."

"Then why so quiet?"

She pursed her lips as if trying to determine what to say. "Well, truthfully... I've enjoyed today, but I conveniently forgot that you were here such a short time. It's not like it's something I haven't known all along."

"Does that mean you'd like me to stay?" he asked, even knowing he never could. The last thing he wanted was to set up some false expectation that he might. He wasn't the kind of guy to commit to personal relationships, and he would never want to hurt her. Still, he wanted to know the answer. Her opinion mattered, and that was a rare thing for him.

She looked up at him. "If I say yes, don't read too much into it. I know in a lot of ways we're very different, but you like some of the same things I do. And you seem to like me, even though I'm..."

She broke off, her cheeks flamed. He could tell, even in the hot sun, that she was embarrassed. He touched her hand and asked gently, "Even though you're what?"

The answer was a long time coming; they skirted around a group of Japanese tourists and then past a dog walker with five dogs on leashes, all of which were amenable to pats and lots of "good boys." He wondered if she was going to answer at all when she spoke softly.

"I've always been the tomboy type. I'm not curvy or exceptionally pretty, not like Adele. I usually have a hard time making friends. And as much as I know starting something between us would be a mistake, I also know it's been nice to feel...wanted."

An ache settled in around his heart. Harper was lonely, and loneliness was something he understood.

"You can have lots of friends and still be lonely," he admitted. They were walking in the direction of her house, and he didn't mind. The ice cream had kept him from being hungry for a late lunch, and there was nothing in the commercial part of town that he was dying to go to today.

"I can't believe you're lonely," she said, glancing over at him. "You're so outgoing and driven and..."

"And I miss my family a lot. I have friends but a lot of my relationships are ones of utility. It's not quite as charming as you'd think." He paused for a moment, reflecting. The words had just come out, but he realized how true they were. "You know, some of the most genuine, rewarding connections I've made have been through travel. A man who takes you to his village and invites you to dinner with his family. A tour guide who stands on the edge of a volcano with you and ponders life's big questions. As much as I love the business, and I do, don't get me wrong, I do occasionally get lonely."

"Wow. Then let me say you do a great job of covering it with charm and confidence."

"I love what I do and I'm good at it. But it doesn't fulfill every single aspect of my life."

They stopped on the sidewalk outside her house. "Nor should it, really. Not if you want any sort of balance."

She was so right. "Then here we are," he said, "two very proficient people who love their jobs, who occasionally miss personal interaction."

"This has been an incredibly deep discussion." Her gaze touched his and then shifted to the house. "I have lemonade or some sparkling water if you're interested in a drink. But I understand if you have to keep going."

He held her gaze and smiled. "If it means I can drink it sitting on that porch with you, I'm in."

CHAPTER SEVEN

HARPER'S PULSE WAS drumming rapidly as she poured two glasses of lemonade and carried them out to the front porch. The overhang of the porch roof kept them shaded, but the afternoon was warm and mellow and perfect for sitting and enjoying the weather. That she would be sitting with Drew was what had her in a tizzy.

Because he'd kissed her today, and it had been lovely. Wonderful, even. More tender than she'd expected; gentle and unhurried. They'd had a simple ice cream in the sun and he'd held her hand. She'd had to pull away before she got too used to it, because it made her feel so lovely and special and she didn't want to read too much into anything. Next thing she'd start actually caring, and then have her heart crushed beneath his heel.

She handed him his lemonade and remembered the look on his face when he admitted he was lonely.

"Thanks," he said easily, and they sat on the porch swing together, a good twelve inches between them. He took a sip and leaned back, closing his eyes. "This is perfect. Reminds me of home a little."

Home. There wasn't any compliment that would have meant more to her. She'd been in Banff for several years now; longer than she could ever remember being in one place since she was a little girl. She'd put down her own roots and she loved her little house.

"I'm sure your folks had a much bigger house and yard."

He laughed. "They did. There were four of us kids, and a couple of pets usually. But there was something about it, even in all the chaos, that was calming. I don't know. I guess we always knew we were welcomed."

She swallowed against a lump in her throat. "You're welcome here, Drew."

"Thanks."

He nudged his toe on the floor and set the swing moving a little, a lazy back-and-forth that lulled. The lemonade was cool and tart, the sun warm and lazy, and Harper closed her eyes for a moment, breathing in the scent of a neighbour's fresh-cut grass and the spicy smell of the geraniums in her porch planters.

She opened her eyes slowly and saw Drew grinning at her. "What?"

"You look like you could go to sleep."

"Sorry. I'm really relaxed."

He put his drink down on a patio table and leaned toward her. Her heartbeat quickened, but he didn't touch her. Instead he reorganized the pillows on the swing so she could lean back along the side. "Here. Turn around and rest your head there, and put your feet on my lap."

The accelerated heartbeat made her chest squeeze tighter and she shook her head. "Oh, I'm fine, don't be silly."

"When was the last time you took a few hours off and had a nap? Seriously. I'm going to drink my lemonade and wait for my phone to buzz, so please."

She was tired. Pregnancy had a way of doing that to her and the indulgence was so tempting. "I'm not going to sleep. But it would be nice to put my feet up."

It took only ten seconds for her to put her nearly empty glass on the table, shift sideways and lean back against the plump cushions, and for Drew to settle her feet across his lap, his arm lying casually across her shins. "Better?"

It was more than better. It was heaven.

And then he set the swing moving with his toe, just a little, and she closed her eyes. The warm breeze kissed her skin; she listened to the birds singing and the wind fluttering the leaves of the trees. Drew's phone buzzed and he shifted a little to respond, but said nothing as her breath deepened. She put her hand over her belly, thinking about the little life inside her that was causing all these changes, and the fact that Drew seemed remarkably unfazed that she was carrying his niece or nephew.

That was her last thought until she woke, her feet still in Drew's lap. He had nodded off, too, his phone still cradled in his hand, and she took a moment to look at him without fear of being caught.

There was so much more to him than she'd imagined. Things that were so good and made her think they had a lot in common, and then things that showed her how different they were. He came from a big happy family; she was an only child who'd been abandoned and then adopted. He had wandering feet; she longed to put down roots. She lived from check to check, putting whatever she could back into her business after paying the rent; he was a successful businessman.

And yet despite his ambition and energy, there were things they had in common, too. A love of the outdoors. Loneliness, sure, but also an appreciation for the people who embraced them and were important, like Adele and Dan. Ice cream and lemonade and quiet afternoons on a front porch now and then. Naps.

His lashes lay on the crests of his cheeks, his lips slightly open. She sighed as she remembered those lips on hers, so beguiling. She was still in awe that he seemed to find her attractive. Most men found her...plain. Or friend material, someone good for a laugh but not as a love interest. Or, like Jared, they found her disposable. Good for a while but not exciting enough to hang on to.

But Drew, with his shaggy hair and dancing eyes, made her feel special.

Maybe she should enjoy that while she could. He'd already said he'd be leaving soon, once the details on the property were signed. He had a number of other stores to run, after all. But for a few weeks...

She closed her eyes again, just for a moment, and let herself imagine what it would be like if this was real life. If he were a husband and she were a wife and this was their baby. And this was their porch and a stolen afternoon together, with the bees buzzing around and the birds singing in the trees. It filled her heart with an ache so sharp she nearly caught her breath.

She wanted that kind of life, and if her past dating history was any indication, she might never have it. She tended to have a lot of first and second dates, but after that either she decided they weren't for her or they moved on. Yeah, she was cautious— who wouldn't be? So when men told her she was "cold" or "too guarded," she figured they weren't willing to put in the effort.

She certainly hadn't come close to anything like she'd had with Jared, and that had been a farce from the beginning. The closest she might get was this moment, right now. The stolen kiss this afternoon and a nap on the front porch in the sunlight. She tucked both memories into her heart for safekeeping.

A snuffle came from the other end of the swing and she opened her eyes again. Drew was waking, his dark eyes slightly unfocused and a sheepish smile on his face. "I guess I nodded off along with you."

"It's cozy. Did you hear from the agent?"

"We're countering. I'm expecting another call soon."

She nodded but still didn't move to sit up. Once she did, the moment would be truly gone. Right now his hand was rubbing absently on her ankle. She wasn't even sure he knew he was doing it, but it felt incredible and she wasn't in any hurry for him to stop.

"Do you find yourself sleepy a lot with the pregnancy?"

She was surprised at the question, and nodded a little. "Yeah. Not bone tired all the time, but there are definitely times when I think I could easily go for a nap. Like today. Why do you ask?"

His thumb rubbed behind her anklebone. *Ahhhh.*

"I might have googled a bit."

She laughed. "Really?"

"Really. After you were sick the other day, I wondered. You women go through a lot to have kids."

"That's...kind of sweet of you."

His thumb stopped circling, but his hand wrapped around her ankle reassuringly. "You're carrying my niece or nephew, and putting your body through all of these changes for someone else. That's pretty damned selfless. I guess I never really thought about the small things that would affect you. What's been the hardest so far?"

She thought about it for a moment, wondering if she dare speak the truth. He was Dan's brother. What if she spilled and he went back to Dan and told him what she said? Trust didn't come easily to her, but she trusted Adele and that was where her loyalty lay.

But she hesitated too long, and he leaned over a little, examining her face. "What is it? Is there something wrong?"

"No, of course not," she replied. "We had an appointment earlier in the week and everything is great. We got to hear the heartbeat."

"I heard!" He smiled and straightened, then his face fell. "You don't look thrilled. What's going on?"

"If I tell you, I'm going to sound like the worst person alive."

"I doubt it. But try me."

She swallowed against a lump in her throat. "I shouldn't be surprised that I feel…attached. I mean, I knew that would happen when I offered to do this. I also thought that I would remind myself that I'm just the incubator, that the baby is Dan and Adele's. Intellectually I know that's true. Emotionally I'm finding it harder than I expected. Hearing the heartbeat made it so real. There's a little human inside of me, Drew, and I find that wonderful and surreal and overwhelming. It's a little odd. I made all these assurances to Dan and Adele that they'd be involved every step of the way, but when we heard the heartbeat and they were celebrating, it was me who felt left out."

She let out a huge breath. "And I'm totally aware how selfish that sounds. Why should I feel left out?"

"Because you're human. I'm sorry, Harper."

"Don't be sorry. Like I said, intellectually, I know this is going to work out how it should—with Dan and Adele having a beautiful baby. But if I feel this attached now, how will I feel when he or she starts kicking? Or when they are born?" She thought about her own adoptive mother and sighed. "My mom always said motherhood was more about heart than biology. I'm finding it hard not to think of myself as a mother. Sometimes I think I need to protect myself from having these feelings somehow."

He didn't say anything, and when the silence drew out, she admitted, "And who knows if I'll ever have my own?"

Drew sat up straighter and puckered his eyebrows. "Why wouldn't you? You're not even thirty yet. You have lots of time."

"Maybe, but call me old-fashioned—I'd like to be settled with a partner before having kids, and that doesn't seem to be on the horizon anytime soon. Hasn't ever been, actually."

"What are you talking about?"

She shrugged, pulled her legs off his lap and sat up. "I've always been something of a tomboy, you know? And I don't make friends easily. I tend to fade into the woodwork. Which is fine." She tried not to sound defensive; after all, she'd chosen to hold back to avoid getting hurt time and time again when she would inevitably have to move. "I'm just more comfortable behind a camera than in front of it."

"Too tomboyish? A wallflower?" His face had blanked, as if he truly didn't understand. But she knew it was the truth. She still felt all the times that girls had been asked to dances and on dates and she'd been overlooked. Or how her mom had taken her prom dress shopping and they'd bought a beautiful gown, only she hadn't found a date.

That marked the one and only time she'd lied to her mom. She'd got ready, let her mom take some pictures at the house, and then had said she was going to a friend's place as several of them were going without dates.

Instead she'd gone to a nearby lake with a book and a stash of sodas in the car. And she'd gone home at nine thirty, telling her mom she'd had a great time, but that she felt a migraine coming on from the lights and music and she was going to bed.

Then Jared had come along, and she'd fallen hard. Only to have her heart spectacularly broken. Was it any wonder she was a bit jaded?

She wouldn't say any of that to Drew, though. There was sharing and then there was oversharing. It was easier to stick to the plain Jane theory.

"I'm an outdoor girl," she explained. "I don't wear makeup much. I don't know, I guess I don't… stand out. I'm kind of invisible. Which is fine—I'm happy not being the center of attention." It had served her well, all the times she'd moved to a new town and been the "new girl."

"But it might be nice to be the center of someone's attention?"

That he articulated it so well caused a pang in her chest. "Well, yeah, I guess."

"Harper?"

"Hmm?"

He looked her fully in the face. "You've got my attention now."

Oh my. She surely did. He wasn't smiling, wasn't cracking a joke or trying to be deliberately charming. He was being truthful and focusing all his attention on her.

"Do you want to know what I see?"

"I'm not sure if I do or not."

A ghost of a smile flirted with his lips. "I'm going to tell you anyway. I see a woman who is caring and generous. I see someone who is beautiful and doesn't realize it. Who doesn't need makeup and who has the sweetest little blanket of freckles over her nose. I see a body strong from walking trails and climbing rocks and streams to get a perfect photo of a baby bear cub. I see that same strong body growing a new life for someone who can't. Don't ever say you're plain or ordinary again."

Tears burned in her eyes at his earnest words. They weren't like his compliments at the wedding, engineered to woo and romance. They were heartfelt and sincere and she loved him for them, even if she wasn't *in* love with him.

His phone buzzed but he didn't look down at it. He held her gaze until she gave a sniff and a small nod. "That's the sweetest thing anyone has ever said to me."

"If that's true, it's a damned shame." He smiled then. "People should be appreciated and told so."

"How did you get so wise?" she asked, blinking away the last of the moisture from her eyes. She wasn't going to weep over his sweet words, even if they'd touched her deeply.

"My father. We're very quick to criticize when someone does something we don't like. But we hold on to our compliments and praise, and it doesn't make sense." He scowled a little bit, and she wondered if she was thinking about anyone in particular. "It's the biggest life lesson I've taken with me," he continued, "and it's probably the number one thing that's helped me in business, too."

Business. Right. The comparison took a little of the bloom off the rose of his compliment, but it also made her respect him even more. For all his charm, she was starting to realize his success came from a place of very hard work and genuinely appreciating his people. It was an attractive quality for sure. One that spoke of integrity.

"Your phone buzzed, by the way," she offered softly.

"I know. I'll get to it. I want to make sure you're okay first. You're not invisible, Harper. I promise."

Her gaze slipped away and she focused on a bumblebee that was sitting comfortably in the middle of a clump of blue lobelia in one of her planters. His words—*you're not invisible*—left her with an odd feeling of discomfort. Did she want to be invisible? Maybe. And if she did, then how could she really complain about being alone? Deep down, she knew she'd made a habit of pushing people away. If she didn't let herself care too much, then it wouldn't hurt when they inevitably moved on.

"I'm okay. Really. I've just been holding that inside for a while."

"Because you'd normally tell Adele, and this time you can't."

She nodded, an ache around her heart.

"Then I'm glad I was here."

"Please don't say anything to Dan or Adele. They're so excited about the baby and they're my best friends. I wouldn't hurt them for the world."

"Of course I won't. But…" A smile curved his lips as he tapped a few buttons on his phone. "Guess what I have on here?"

She frowned a little, curious. "What?"

He tapped another button and leaned closer to her, smiling. A steady *bah bum, bah bum* sounded from his speakers. Her heart gave a little leap. "You have the heartbeat?"

"Dan sent it to me, dying to share it. And now you can hear it, too."

The steady, quick sounds of the baby's heartbeat filled the air. She knew the recording would end, but the moment it did, it merely looped again so it started over. She put her hand on her tummy, sucked in a shaky breath. "Oh," she said quietly, feeling that same overwhelming awe that had struck her in the doctor's office.

"Pretty incredible, huh?"

She nodded, unable to erase the smile from her face.

"How do you feel?"

Oh, that he would ask. No one else had really thought to. She was emotionally invested; how could she not be? She swallowed against the tightness in her throat and reached for his hand.

"Humbled," she whispered, letting out a breath. "And powerful at the same time. That little heartbeat…that's in here." She withdrew her hand and pointed at her abdomen.

"Pretty crazy, huh?" He let it play again, and she took his hand and placed it on her belly, which had only the slightest little bump. Not even noticeable if you didn't have previous shape to use as context.

His gaze locked with hers. "That's my niece or nephew in there."

She nodded.

"And still so tiny."

"I know. I'm not even showing yet. But this… this made it all real to me. More than an idea, you know? Thank you, Drew. So much."

"I can forward it to you if you want."

"Would you?"

He nodded and handed over his phone, pulling

his other palm away from her belly. "Go ahead and program your number."

She did and handed it back, then let out a happy sigh. The afternoon was waning, and Drew checked his phone. "They've countered again. We're making one more counteroffer and if he won't come down, the deal's off."

Her mouth dropped open. "Just like that?"

Drew grinned and shrugged. "He'll come down," he said with confidence. "If he doesn't, he doesn't. I think this would be a great location for our first Canadian store, but there are other spots. I'm not going to overpay for real estate."

"You love this, don't you? The bargaining."

"Kind of. What I really love is taking something from scratch and building it, and watching it all come together."

And then moving on to the next challenge. She couldn't forget that. She'd told him before that she wasn't a challenge or a trophy. Now that she knew him better, she knew he didn't see people that way. But it was how he viewed life. Challenges and adventures. In her eyes, a lot of adventures meant confusion and trying to carve a new spot for herself in a strange place with strange people.

Still, he'd listened to her, and he'd given her the moment she'd missed in the doctor's office. He was a good man. A friend, and those were hard to come by.

"Would you like to stay for dinner?" she asked. "I know you're waiting for another update, and I'm an okay cook…for a vegetarian."

"I'd love to."

"You would?" She looked over at him, surprised. She'd half expected him to decline, since they'd spent all afternoon together.

He laughed. "Don't act so surprised. I'm staying in a hotel. I have to eat most of my meals out or suck up to Dan and Adele." He leaned over a bit, enough that she could smell his shampoo, something outdoorsy and fresh. "Little secret. I'm a decent cook. I can even help."

"Well, all right, then." She grinned and pushed on her knees, getting up from the swing. "How do you feel about pad thai?"

"I have very warm feelings about it, actually."

She grinned and led the way inside, taking her glass with her, and he followed, bringing his own nearly gone and now-warm lemonade. She got them new glasses and poured them each a glass of water, then stood across from him at the kitchen island. "So. Do you want to chop vegetables or tofu?"

Drew slid the knife through the carrots and stole a glance at Harper, who was dropping cubes of tofu into a pan with hot oil. It sizzled and spattered a little, and she slid the pan on the burner to stir the cubes. Water was boiling for the rice noodles, and he watched her move around the kitchen, gathering ingredients for the sauce.

He couldn't believe she ever thought herself invisible. And absolutely couldn't believe that some guy hadn't snapped her up already. Maybe she wasn't the flashiest woman around, and maybe she didn't turn heads on the street. Not because she wasn't beautiful but because…

He suddenly smiled. Because she was a chameleon. He didn't know why, but she blended in with her environment no matter where she was.

"How are the carrots and onions?"

He gave a few more chops and finished up the carrot. "Good. Is this fine enough?" He angled the cutting board for her approval.

"Perfect." She took the board from him and slid the vegetables into the pan with the now-crispy tofu, then went back to work whisking ingredients together for the sauce.

It was a domestic type of scene he was unused to. His "dates" usually consisted of restaurants and plus-one type of events. Definitely not comfy home-cooked meals and lemonade on a swing.

It had been different—once. A few years ago he'd fallen in love but she wanted the kind of life he didn't, and the type of commitment he couldn't give. In the end he'd hurt her, badly, even though breaking it off had been the right thing to do. These days he didn't make promises he couldn't keep. Being with Harper sometimes made him forget that, and he had to keep his guard up when he started feeling too comfortable.

She had him crush peanuts courtesy of two pieces of parchment paper and a rolling pin. In no time at all she'd fixed two bowls, sprinkled his crushed peanuts on top and led the way to the dining table, which was little more than a café table with two chairs in the somewhat small kitchen.

He carried their water glasses, and before long they were seated across from each other and sharing the meal.

She told him about working with Juny and her plans to have her take over more jobs; he shared his ideas for the store and then they both threw around ideas for renovation. He ate the spicy noodles and marveled at the way her eyes shone when she grew animated, or waved her fork around—empty, of course—when she talked with her hands. He refilled water glasses and laughed when she cracked a joke about pregnant womens' bladder capacity. They finished and he helped her load the dishwasher and then wash up the few pots and pans. When he was drying the last dish, her phone buzzed, vibrating loudly against the countertop.

"I'll finish this," Drew said, wiping his hands on the dish towel. "Go ahead and answer it."

She picked up the phone. "Oh, hi, Adele. No,

I'm not busy." She looked over at Drew and rolled her eyes, and he laughed.

But then the humor faded from her face. "Oh. Oh, I see. Okay. Well, if you're ready, of course." She took a deep breath and met Drew's gaze. "Hey, we knew you were going to start telling people eventually. You must be so excited."

There was a long pause where Adele had to be speaking, and Harper smiled a little, and then said, "Don't worry about me. And don't worry about what anyone else thinks, either, okay? Remember how quickly Drew was on board. And you can message me later. Good luck."

She hung up the phone. "Dan and Adele are telling your family tonight and wanted to give me the heads-up."

"Oh. Are you okay with that?"

She shrugged. "Why wouldn't I be? I mean, it was their decision and their baby and it's Dan's family."

"Except you think they'll be skeptical, as I was?"

She laughed a little and leaned back against the counter. "That lasted all of about five minutes. If your family is like you, it'll be fine."

"You're right."

"Do you want some tea?"

It appeared as if she was letting it go, but he could tell she was still a little anxious. He seriously didn't know what to say.

They were halfway through their tea when his phone buzzed. And in the space of two breaths, it went off twice more.

Harper looked over at him. "You should probably check it. You're still waiting for news, remember?"

Funny how he'd nearly forgotten about the real estate offer. His jaw tightened as he reached for his phone. Instead of the agent, it was messages from his two sisters. At least they seemed excited, with a side order of "OMG can you believe they did this?"

Then came the message from his mother, and it wasn't quite so generous.

His parents were of a more traditional variety, and his mother had tons of questions about "this Harper woman" and what she was after. He fired back a quick response, but he'd honestly hoped for better. His mother, especially, had always been accepting and kind. He understood she was being a protective mom, but he reminded her that she was going to be a grandmother again and that Harper was Adele's best friend and not some stranger.

But it sat wrong with him.

"Your family?" she asked quietly.

"There's no sense lying, is there?"

She shook her head, her gaze steady. "Not a bit."

"It'll be fine. My parents are more traditional, I suppose. It's a generation-gap kind of thing."

"That was the last text, wasn't it?" Her lips tightened, and he was truly angry at his mother for being anything less than supportive.

"Do they think what you thought that first night?" she asked, standing perfectly still in the middle of her tiny kitchen. "That I'm in it for something? That I'm after money or…" She swallowed again.

"I don't know." He figured not telling her would be worse than being honest. "Listen, all she said was to ask if I'd known about this and did I actually think it was a good idea." She'd also asked what kind of woman would agree to carry someone else's baby. He'd bet fifty bucks that her solution would have been to adopt or get a dog, not go through a bunch of medical testing or a uterus-for-rent.

He softened his expression and went to her. "Hey, listen, it's okay. Mom's in shock. No one knew Dan and Adele were even considering such a thing, you know? And the girls…they'll be super supportive. They have kids of their own." He took her hands in his and gave them a little shake.

"Supportive of Dan and Adele. Who knows what they think of me?"

"Within two minutes of talking to you, they'll think exactly as I do. That you're a wonderful, generous, loving person. Mom and Dad will, too. They're good and fair people."

Harper let out a breath. "Okay."

"And besides, you're not doing this for them. You're doing it for Adele."

"Yeah," she said, and she tried a wobbly smile.

"Forget *my* family," he said sternly. "Who do you want to tell? Who do you want to share this news with?"

Her eyes widened. "Oh. Uh. Well, Juny. It's been horrible keeping this from her when she's at the studio all the time."

"Then you should call her. Or invite her over. Who else?"

The tears came back in her eyes and one leaked over her lashes and down her cheek. "My mom. I'm adopted, you see. She'll understand how Adele's feeling and how I'm feeling. It's been so hard doing this without telling my mom."

He led her into the living room and what appeared to be her most comfortable chair. Then he gave her her phone and went back to the kitchen to retrieve her tea. "Here. Have your tea and call your mom." He got a light blanket off the sofa and put it over her legs. "Curl up and be comfortable and celebrate what you're doing, sweetheart. It's a wonderful thing. Don't let anyone take it away from you."

She looked up at him with wide, luminous eyes. "Don't go."

He knew he should, but he nodded. "I won't. I'll go out on the porch and give you some privacy and see where we're at with the building purchase. Okay?"

She nodded. He smiled and started for the hall, when her voice stopped him.

"Drew?"

He turned around.

"Thank you. For this, and for the support, and for being my friend today."

He'd kissed her. Just now he'd called her *sweetheart* by mistake. He was feeling far more than friendly toward her but this situation called for support and not seduction.

"You're welcome," he said simply, and went to the front porch to take care of some business.

CHAPTER EIGHT

HARPER FOUND HIM sitting on the porch swing again, an ankle crossed over his knee as he scrolled through something on his phone.

He'd been right. Calling her mom had been just what she needed. She'd wait and tell Juny tomorrow before work. Maybe she'd take in tea and scones or something. In any case, the news was out, and she was free of any big secret. After Drew's unconditional support and her mother's excitement and love, there was a contentment in her heart that had been missing for most of her pregnancy.

"Did you make the sale?" she asked softly.

He looked up and smiled. "I did. And you look much better."

"My eyes are red from crying a bit."

"Yeah, but you look happier. More relaxed."

She went to the swing and sat down. "I am."

When he opened his arm along the top of the swing, she accepted the invitation and leaned into his embrace. She'd desperately needed the touch of another human being lately, and Drew was warm and strong and reassuring.

"I'm glad. I talked to my mom, too, by the way. And gave her an earful."

Harper pushed against his ribs, moving to sit up. "You didn't. Oh, Drew. I wish you hadn't."

"Don't you worry. I told her that you were a wonderful friend doing a wonderful thing and to insinuate anything more was totally off base. And then I reminded her that this meant another grandchild to spoil and told her to get with the times."

"You played into her weakness."

"Nonsense. I prefer to think that I reminded her of the benefits of this arrangement and that ultimately you were helping her to get what she and Dad want most. Lots of little Brimicombes running around."

"Which conveniently gets you off the hook."

"For the time being. As the one kid with no children, it'll come back around." He chuckled. "Come back here and relax a bit more. I got the building for eight percent over my first offer, and we'll sign the purchase agreement tomorrow."

"That means you'll be leaving soon."

"Oh, another week or so. There's lots to do here. I'm going to hire a local team to do the renos, and it's short notice so a lot of companies are probably already booked for the fall. There are things for me to do here, don't worry."

"I'm happy for you."

"Me, too. When I first got here, I had nothing

but expansion on my mind. But coming back home to Canada…it feels really good. I can't lie about it."

She leaned against his ribs and sighed. "I didn't think you wanted a home. More of a home base."

"I was speaking in more general terms. Sacramento is my home base, I guess. I'm not there much."

She smiled against him. It wasn't his fault she'd been bounced around as a kid and had struggled to make friends. Maybe it was easier to move around when you were an adult if you'd had more stability as a kid.

"You're an adventurer at heart," she said. "I love how you own it." Even if it meant he was going to be in her life such a brief time and then out of it again.

"That doesn't mean I don't enjoy days like today, Harper. It's been very nice sharing it with you. Thank you for going with me this afternoon. For dinner. Heck, for the ice cream."

For the kiss. The words sat on her tongue but she didn't say them.

Drew was leaving soon. The difference between now and her past hurtful encounter was that she knew it and had no unreasonable expectations. She was under no illusions that this was forever or he was The One. There was a certain level of protection in that.

So she tilted her head up slightly and met his

gaze, then blinked slowly, wondering if he was interested in a continuation of this afternoon's sweet kiss.

"Harper," he said softly, a note of caution in his voice.

"I know. I know I said no in March. And I'm not looking for a wild and torrid affair. But I don't want to pretend I'm not attracted to you, Drew. I know you're leaving. It's okay."

"Damn," he murmured, lifting his hand and placing it along her cheek. "You don't know what you're asking."

"I'm not asking for anything. I'm saying when your business in town is done, you're walking away and I'm fine with it. Maybe I have been trying too hard to be invisible. You see me, and it makes me…a little bit brave."

Her heart was pounding from the vulnerability in that admission. But then his fingers grazed her jaw and his eyes darkened as they looked deeply into hers.

"Let's go inside," he said, his voice low and rough. "Because if I kiss you, I want to do it right, and not in view of your neighbours."

Her body got a little thrill from those dark and promising words, and she stood up from the swing, her knees shaking a little. She led the way inside, her insides quaking with nervousness and anticipation.

She got three steps inside the hallway when he reached out and grabbed her hand, stopping her. His gaze caught hers, dark and full of purpose in the early evening light. He took a step closer, and another, while an army of butterflies took flight in her belly. Her tongue snuck out to wet her lips… oh Lord, had he just noticed that? One more step and his body was so close to hers that she took a step back and found herself against the wall. The screen door was barely a meter away. Moments ago they'd been mere friends. If he kissed her now— and surely he was going to—it would change everything.

He stepped closer still, so her back was pressed against the wall and his chest and hips lightly grazed her denim skirt and blouse. Her breath came short and fast, her lips parted. And still he held her gaze, darkly, deeply, until his mouth was only a few inches from hers and her lashes fluttered closed.

Like this afternoon, he kissed the side of her mouth first, a feather-soft graze of warm lips to tender skin. She let out a breath and tried hard not to moan in response, but kept her eyes closed, enjoying the kiss with all her other senses. He ran his lips to her jaw, then below her ear, causing a shiver that ran straight down her spine. Then the corner of her eyebrow, the tip of her nose, the delicate dip above her frenulum. "Drew," she breathed, realizing that her arms hung limply at her sides. She wasn't able to do anything right now but *feel*.

But her plea did the trick. He placed his hands on the wall on either side of her head and leaned in, covering her mouth with his, a full kiss that had her body responding automatically with a whimper and her arms lifting to coil around his torso.

Subtle head movements, dips and nips and low sounds of encouragement kept the kiss going for a long, long time. It had been years since Harper had been kissed this thoroughly, if ever. Drew's fit body pressed against hers, all muscled chest and lean hips that translated his desire. But still he kept everything at the kissing stage. It didn't matter. When one was an expert, there was no need to rush to the next level.

"You taste good," he murmured, running his lips over to her ear again. She gasped and he chuckled, low and sexy, by her ear. "Told you I wanted to do it right."

She ran her hand over his shoulder. "You really are an overachiever."

"Thank you." His tongue skimmed along to the curve of her neck and she really wondered how far they could go tonight.

His hand left the wall and skimmed down her neck, two fingertips tracing a trail to her collarbone.

He kissed her again, this time with more urgency, and their bodies responded in kind. When it was clear they either had to stop or take things to a whole other level, Drew backed away, breathing heavily.

"You definitely did it right," she said, her voice low with pleasure. "My whole body is humming right now."

"Be careful saying things like that. I'm likely to ask you to show me where your bedroom is."

"And I'm tempted to take you there."

"But we shouldn't."

"We shouldn't."

A long moment held between them, as if each was deliberating the pros and cons.

"You," he said quietly, "are a very tempting woman, and whoever made you feel otherwise is a damned fool."

"Fools," she corrected, but smiled at him, still feeling rather boneless. "And I might have a hard time believing you, but I believe that you mean it, so that's something."

"You're so confident about everything else. I don't know why you're so sure you're unexceptional. But I have a week or so to try to convince you you're amazing."

And then he did something so unexpected that she didn't know what to say or do. He stepped forward and placed his palm on her abdomen. "This is amazing. I mean, the sheer biology of it alone is miraculous but that you would do this for another person…you have a huge, wonderful heart, Harper. You do. Don't let anyone make you feel small."

He kissed her again, a small, tender kiss, with his hand still on her stomach.

"You struck me as such a player," she finally murmured. "But you're not. You're an observant, considerate man with a lot of integrity behind all that charm. In another time or place…"

"We might have fallen in love?"

Love. Her heart jolted at even the mention of the word and she took a mental step backward. "Maybe. But not now. Now we…" She couldn't come up with the right words.

"Enjoy each other's company, and accept that when the time comes, we go our separate ways with best wishes and good memories. No regrets."

"You said that so well it makes me think you've done it before."

"I've done it, but it didn't end well," he replied, his gaze serious. "I broke someone's heart and hated myself for it. But I couldn't live a lie, and the kind of life she wanted wasn't for me. I like you, Harper. More than that, I admire you. So maybe we can admire each other for a few more days, and leave things with fond memories. It's all I can offer and you should know that up front."

Why not? she thought. It would be a definite change of pace from her other romantic experiences. She'd lost her virginity when she was twenty-one and tired of carrying the burden of it around, and it had been a mediocre experience and certainly not one with any depth of emotion. Her other partner had been Jared. She'd thought him everything she wanted, and he'd disappeared with barely a "see ya." He hadn't even asked for the ring back. It had been disposable, just like her.

Leaving things with happy, "that one summer" sort of memories seemed pretty attractive.

"Does this mean you want to go with me to Healy Pass on Thursday?"

"I'd love to."

"I'll pack food for the day. You know to dress accordingly. It's a longer hike than what we went on the other day, but ten times as rewarding."

"It sounds perfect."

It really did. And the idea of doing the hike with company, and someone who enjoyed the outdoors as much as she did? Heaven.

"I suppose this means I should go for now."

"You can stay if you want to."

"Tempting as that sounds, I feel like I've already overstayed my welcome. But thank you for dinner, and for everything."

"Anytime." And she meant it.

He let go of her hands and turned to go to the door, but paused when he got there. "I'll pick you up Thursday morning. How does that sound?"

"Perfect."

He was holding open the door, but he let it go and walked back inside, coming over to plant a final kiss on her lips. "That's better," he said, and then went for the door. "See you Thursday."

When he was gone, Harper went into the living room and sat down in her favorite chair. Half of her tea was still in her mug and cold now, but it didn't matter.

The people who mattered most knew about the baby. And Drew had kissed her. Twice. More than twice when she thought about it. And touched her. And he'd been kind and understanding.

Never in her life had she felt so accepted by a man.

"Oh, Harper," she said to herself. "You're going to have to be very careful."

The following morning she told Juny about the baby. For a moment, the younger woman's eyes widened, and then she sat back with a victorious smile. "Okay, so I *knew* there was something going on with you! No Friday night wine and chocolate plans, and no more morning muffins and coffee on Wednesdays. Plus you looked sickly some of the time. I can't believe you didn't tell me."

But she didn't look hurt, and for that Harper was relieved. "I couldn't. We really wanted to make sure I got past the first trimester before saying anything to anyone. The only person who knew was Drew, and that was because he showed up and I was at Dan and Adele's. He kind of guessed something was up and Dan told him."

"Is that why he's been around lately? Are you guys a thing?" She put extra emphasis on the word *thing*.

Even though Harper felt her face heat, she shook her head. "No, we're not a thing. We've hung out a few times over the past couple of weeks, but that's it."

Juny waggled her eyebrows. "If that was it, you wouldn't be blushing."

Would a half-truth suffice? She sighed and relented a little. "Okay, so I'm not blind. He's very cute and it turns out he's quite nice as well, once you get past that veneer of charm."

"I bet."

"Shut up. How are things with you and Renée?"

"Fine, and don't change the subject. I've known you for two years now and I've never seen you blush over a guy. In fact, other than mentioning the odd one-off date, I don't think I've seen you talk about guys at all."

Harper took a sip of tea, decaf Earl Grey this time since she no longer relied on mint tea to settle her stomach. "I'm not a social butterfly, you know that. My friend circle is pretty small, so it's been kind of nice."

"I'll let you off the hook for now."

"Thank you so much," she replied, sarcasm ripe in her voice but accompanied by a smile. "Have another scone. There's a chocolate chunk one in there somewhere."

"Bless you." Juny rooted around in the bag until she came up with the scone, then broke it in half and gave a piece to Harper. "So how is this going to work with the studio?"

"I'm glad you asked." Harper gave her the rundown on her plans to include Juny in more photo shoots, so that she could take on some of the photography duties as the pregnancy advanced. "I'm not booking anything after New Year's," she said. "I'm due in January, and I don't want to leave anyone stranded. Right now we only have one date in November and one in December, but that'll change. I think you and I should consult together on any late-year jobs that come up and decide if we can take them. But I'm not taking much time off after the baby is born. I'm going to need to get back to work and into a regular schedule."

Juny's dark eyes took on a concerned expression. "Are you afraid, Harper? I mean, you're going through all this and then handing the baby over. I know you said genetically it's Dan and Adele's, but this isn't an easy thing."

Harper nodded. "Yeah, I'm a little afraid. So I don't want to set myself up to mope around after it's over. I'll get to spoil this baby rotten." She put her hand on her tummy. "Anyway, if you're okay with a few extra weekend hours doing events with me, I thought I'd look at hiring someone part time to work the storefront." It would mean being even more disciplined with the finances, but if Juny worked out as Harper hoped, they could take on more bookings in the new year to balance out the extra cost of another staff member.

"I'd love that."

"I can spare some extra equipment for now when we go out together. But if it's a tentative plan moving forward, we can figure it out as we go."

"Sounds fine to me. You can pay me in chocolate chunk scones." Juny brushed some crumbs off her lap.

Then she looked up at Harper and smiled. "I'm only going to say one more thing about Drew. Yesterday, when you came out of the back room and he was waiting, you looked so happy. I've never seen you look quite that way before. Even if you're just hanging out until he goes back to wherever, he's good for you. So enjoy yourself."

The support sent a warm feeling through Harper, and she felt very blessed with her friendships. They weren't great in number, but quality-wise they were top-notch.

"Thanks," she said, trying not to look too happy and sure she was failing. The memory of last night's kiss still made her stomach tangle in delicious knots. "And speaking of, I'm taking him on a day hike up to Healy Pass tomorrow. We'll be out of range so I'll be back in the studio on Friday morning. I have the MacPherson rehearsal on Friday night."

"Sounds fine. Now I'd better get out there and unlock the doors. I sold three of the five-by-sevens yesterday, by the way. Maybe next week you can pick some new photos for prints and we can shuffle some stuff around out front. It's the perfect size for tourists who want something for their luggage."

"I'll pick a few and match some mattes and frames. Which ones sold?"

"One was a Peyto Lake, and I think the other was Bow Lake. An eight-by-ten of Lake Louise went earlier this week, too."

They were recognizable landmarks, and they did tend to sell well, though Harper knew she had equally good photos of more obscure locations. Maybe there was something to what Drew had said about greeting cards. A good portion of their foot traffic was tourists, and smaller did sell better when it came to transport. It didn't make a lot of sense to turn down an opportunity for sales just because they were a more "disposable" form of her work.

"I'll put some stuff together today and double-check the details for Friday's rehearsal party. Do you want to come with?"

"We close at six. I can meet you after that, if it's local."

"It is."

With the day's plan solidified, Juny went to the store to open and Harper started going through her to-do list. If she were going to be gone all day tomorrow, she had to have things in order today.

Tomorrow. A whole day with Drew in the outdoors. She couldn't think of a finer idea.

CHAPTER NINE

DREW KNOCKED QUIETLY on the screen door. It was only seven thirty, but they had a fun day ahead of them. He couldn't remember the last time he'd looked forward to something so much. Even Dan's "are you sure you know what you're doing" during their phone call last night couldn't put a damper on his good mood.

He'd come up with a crazy surprise for Harper today. Something that would keep Dan and Adele's worry at bay, and give her a special treat.

Harper came to the door, her face bright and cheery. "Good morning. You're right on time."

"I hope so." He slid his pack off his shoulder and put it down in the entry as he stepped inside. Two days ago he'd kissed her brainless in this very spot, and his body stirred with remembrance. Harper did something to him that he hadn't expected. Something wonderful. It was too bad he had to head back to California late next week.

Or maybe not. It would be too easy to get caught up in her and he didn't want to go with any hurt feelings left behind or misunderstandings. On either of their parts.

"I'm just finishing breakfast. Did you have any?"

"I grabbed a breakfast sandwich at the coffee shop." He patted his belly.

She laughed. "I'm just finishing up. Come in and sit down."

He sat at her table while she bit into her egg sandwich. "You want some juice?" she asked. "Milk?"

"Naw, I'm good. I've got a big water bottle." He grinned. She had no idea that today was going to be more of an adventure than she'd bargained for.

"Me, too, in my bag." She laughed. "You know, there's only a washroom at the trailhead. I'm not sure what's going to happen with my pregnant bladder if I drink that much water over the course of the day."

"I'll stand guard for you," he joked, and was gratified when she grinned around the toast in her mouth, a hint of a dimple denting her cheek.

He watched as she wiped her hands on a napkin and grabbed her glass of orange juice. "You ate a whole sandwich. Morning sickness better?"

"Much," she agreed, and put her plate and glass in the dishwasher. "Mostly now I get the odd wave and it passes. Food's stayed down for five days in a row now."

"That must feel better."

"It does."

He waited while she finished putting her pack together. Right now she wore a light jacket over her T-shirt, with a lightweight hoodie in the pack. Bottles of water, her bear spray and sunscreen all went in the backpack.

"You were planning to carry all that *and* your camera?"

"Pretty much. Slightly smaller lens today, though. My neck and back would kill me if I carried that all day. I'm mostly looking for some meadow shots and panoramas." She looked up. "Wait. You said *were*. How come?"

Dammit. Of course he'd make a slip. He figured he might as well get the ball rolling. "Well, as a matter of fact, I have a bit of a surprise for you this morning."

Her brows lifted. "A surprise? I'm not sure if I like that. I'm not really a surprise kind of woman."

He paused and then went to her and took her hands. "Do you trust me, Harper?"

Confusion mingled with warmth in her eyes. "That's a big question, Drew. Especially for me."

"Then listen to your intuition. What does your gut say? Can you trust me?"

There was a moment's hesitation, and then she nodded slightly. "Yes. For some odd reason, I trust you."

"Then let's put this stuff in my car." He dropped a kiss on her cheek. "You're not going to regret this," he promised.

Harper didn't know if she was going to regret it or not. When she went outside, she stopped short at the sight of his rental. The Range Rover SUV sat square in her driveway. A flipping Range Rover! She looked over at Drew, who wore an amused expression. "Something wrong?" he asked.

"No, nothing." She made her feet move and they stowed her gear in the back. Drew headed east on the highway instead of west. When she opened her mouth to speak, he lifted a finger and shushed her. "Surprise, remember?" he said. "And that means you have to wait. You said you were very patient."

"Not about surprises or not knowing where I'm going," she grumbled, slumping down in the seat that cradled her body perfectly. She trusted Drew, but she'd really wanted to hike up the pass today. With the business being so busy, she didn't get a lot of opportunities and as much as it was fun being with Drew, she didn't want to squander her chance for some new shots for her portfolio.

It wasn't long until she realized where he was headed and her head snapped around to stare at him. "The heliport? Are you crazy?" Her stomach turned over both in excitement and fear. A helicopter? She was a bit thrilled and a lot terrified. "Did I not tell you I was afraid of heights?"

He looked over at her and laughed. "You'll be buckled in and snug as a bug. I promise."

"But..." She bit down on her lip. "I've done enough weddings and events to know that a tour is really expensive, Drew. And I know the building you just bought came at a hefty price. You don't need to do this kind of thing."

"It's the money you're worried about?" He seemed unconcerned. Amused, even.

It *was* expensive, she told herself. And yes, she was terrified. But why on earth would he spend the money on this sort of thing? This car rental alone had to cost a lot. Was he always this careless with his money? "It seems extravagant," she answered, twisting her fingers together. "We were supposed to hike."

"And we're going to," he said. "We're going to get dropped off, hike, and then get picked up again." He met her gaze briefly before turning his attention back to the road. "This way you get the alpine meadows and panoramic views without having to do all the hard climbing."

She wasn't sure what to think. Was he doing it because he was being overprotective and thought she wasn't capable? How could she voice that without being insulting? It was a generous and fun thing he had planned, but Adele and Dan were already making her a bit claustrophobic with their concern. Surely it wasn't an attempt to impress her. She'd never once given him the impression that her head could be turned by such things.

"I'm still capable of doing the hike, you know," she said. "Not that I don't appreciate the gesture, but I'm in great shape. I don't need to be coddled."

They pulled into the parking lot and Drew shut off the engine, then turned to face her. "So hear me out," he said, resting his left hand on the steering wheel. "I don't know if you realize it, but it's not often that I get a day like we had on Tuesday. An afternoon of simple pleasures like a cone of ice cream and a nap on a porch swing. I liked being with you, and I think you liked being with me, and for once it had nothing to do with who I am or…" He ran his hand through his hair. "Or my bank balance, to be honest."

"Why would I care about your bank balance?" Harper puckered her brows. Sure, he had to be successful to have his stores, but Dan and Adele had never said anything about Drew's financial status.

"Most people do," he admitted. "And a lot of the time personal value is determined by the zeroes after your name. But you don't care, do you?"

"I don't even know how much you make," she replied, not quite sure where this was all going. Was he saying he was rich? After all, hiring out a helicopter wasn't something you did when you lived paycheck to paycheck.

"You really don't," he marveled, a smile tugging at his lips. "Harper, my net worth last year was—"

He gave a number that had her lips dropping open and her eyes widening as she gave a very unladylike exclamation.

He chuckled. "So you didn't know. See? This is why I liked being with you. You accepted me at face value. That doesn't happen much anymore."

She was still reeling from the fact that he was a multimillionaire. Drew never put on airs. He wore faded jeans and T-shirts. Drove a pickup, from what he'd said before. He was...ordinary.

But not, she reminded herself. He traveled extensively. Owned a chain of stores. Could apparently rent himself a luxury vehicle and book a custom heli tour at a moment's notice. And he'd hidden that part of himself from her. She was a little bit hurt by that.

"You should have been honest with me," she said, her lips a thin line. "I don't like being lied to, Drew. Or being made a fool of." God, she'd accused him of being extravagant. She felt so stupid.

"That wasn't my intention at all. I just never know who to trust. If someone likes me for me or if they're after some sort of advantage. I thought that if you knew about the money, it wouldn't have been the same. It wasn't meant to deceive you, I promise. I wanted to enjoy being a regular guy. The last week or so I've felt like an ordinary guy again. I kind of lost touch with that side of me."

She understood that, even though she was still embarrassed. After all, she had her own trust issues. How could she be angry at someone for dealing with their issues in their own way?

"So why the helicopter? Why now?"

He reached over and took her hand. "Because I like you. Because I have fun with you, and this is top-notch fun. I can treat you to something because I want to, not because you expect it, and there's something cool about that, you know? So please, come with me. Let's fly over the Rockies, go for a hike, eat lunch in an alpine meadow. There's no one I'd rather do this with."

She couldn't say no to him, and she suspected that would prove to be her biggest downfall. "I'm scared of heights."

"You'll forget all about it when we're in the air and you take in the scenery. Plus you can hold my hand." He wiggled his eyebrows.

"You're incorrigible," she replied, but knew she was about to get into a helicopter and face one of her biggest fears.

At least it wasn't zip-lining in the jungle.

The helicopter ride was frightening at first, but once they were up in the air it was like nothing

Harper had ever experienced. She thought of her father, who had made a career out of flying, and wondered if he felt this same awe every time he looked out his cockpit window. She and Drew were sitting in the back, headsets on, and before long she had her face pressed to the window as the pilot took them on a tour over peaks and through valleys that made her stomach swoop. Puffy clouds dotted a perfect blue sky and made shadows on the brownish-grey mountains. Turquoise glacial lakes dotted the valleys, mineral deposits creating the vivid colours made brighter by the sun's rays.

"Okay?" Drew asked once, and she nodded quickly. He'd been right, of course. Once in the air, the magnificence of the scenery had chased away any lingering fears. It was amazing! And she never would have done it if he hadn't nudged her out of her comfort zone.

The pilot approached a grassy peak and set the helicopter down with barely a bump. Harper's heart beat fast as she unbuckled her seat belt and Drew helped her out of the aircraft, holding her hand and then reaching for their bags. Together they scurried south, away from the rotating blades, and Drew waved the pilot off. He'd be back in two hours to pick them up. In the meantime, they could explore the meadow and valley, take pictures, and eat the picnic he'd had specially prepared by the Cascade kitchens.

Harper had never felt glamorous before, but she did now.

When the helicopter was gone and her ears stopped ringing, she grinned up at Drew. "Well. I didn't faint."

"You were a trooper. Though I thought you were going to lose your breakfast when we landed. You got pretty pale."

"Funny," she mused. "Way up in the air it seems fine. Get within a hundred feet of the ground and my nerves…" She made a zooming motion with her hand.

"Come on. Let's get your camera out so you can take some pictures."

She opened her bag and took out her camera, attached the lens she wanted and zipped it all back up again. "Ready," she said, with a wide smile.

They descended a bit into an alpine meadow and Drew caught his breath. It was stunningly gorgeous. An endless blue sky soared above, punctuated with nearby peaks and swooped with green valleys. While the drop-off spot had been solid rock and sparse brush, the meadow was positively verdant. As they ventured along the trail, he spotted the nodding blue heads of harebells and the spiky blooms of red paintbrush flowers. There were glacier lilies and the more vibrant yellow of alpine buttercups.

Harper had stopped and was fiddling with her camera, setting up for pictures. It was breathtaking. "It's beautiful, isn't it?"

He nodded, not saying anything. Instead he reached into his bag and took out his camera. The point-and-shoot eliminated the need for any complicated settings, but the waterproof and shockproof features meant it stood up to the most rugged of his adventures. There was no reason why he couldn't get his own photos, even if they weren't artistic like Harper's.

They each wandered, looking for good vantage spots and unique shots, until Harper made her way over to him again. "Here," she said, and she took her camera from around her neck. "I won't make it complicated for you. It's on auto and all you have to do is turn the zoom in or out, and shoot."

"Harper. This is your camera. I mean, it's like giving a teenager a Porsche and saying take it for a spin."

She laughed. "Not quite. Besides, you'd tell a kid to put on his seat belt and I'm telling you to keep that strap around your neck."

He chuckled. "Yes, boss."

"Now go have some fun."

"You're sure?"

"When I first picked up a camera, I didn't want a long lesson about what everything meant. I wanted to look through the lens and frame my shot. I wanted to play. The rest came later, when I fell in love with it and wanted to learn how to be better. Today's your day for playing." She touched his arm. Then she leaned up and placed a kiss on his cheek.

He obeyed, because he was amazed at the level of trust she'd put in him, and he was humbled by what she'd shared. His first few shots were of the wide expanse of the meadow, getting a feel for the heavy instrument in his hands.

But then he took pictures of her. Walking down the path, her pack on her back. The way she turned and her ponytail bobbed from the hole in the back of her ball cap. She didn't go far before she found a large rock and sat upon it, taking off the pack and rolling her shoulders. He was patient—he remembered her saying that patience was important—and got what he felt was a perfect shot of her relaxing on the rock, one booted foot on the grey stone, her arms resting across her knee as she took a breather, looking off into the distance.

It had been two weeks and a handful of encounters, and yet…he felt a strange, uncomfortable stirring in his chest. He was falling for her, he realized. And not because she was so pretty or that they had the outdoors in common, though that certainly helped. It was who she was on the inside. Vulnerable and yet trusting. Easygoing and yet with a perfectionist side he saw each time he viewed one of her photos. She had a quick sense of humor and a ready smile, and a bigger sense of adventure than she gave herself credit for. If there was anything that he didn't like, it was that she seemed really insecure about her personal relationships. He supposed being bounced around as an air force kid would do that, but he got the feeling there was something more, too. Something she hadn't shared with him. He could hardly ask her to when they both knew his place in her life was temporary. It wasn't like he'd shared his deepest secrets, either.

She looked over, her eyes shaded by the brim of the ball cap, but her smile bright and warm. When he was with her things seemed to fall into place. Which was weird, because he already had the life he wanted.

Didn't he?

That he questioned it at all troubled him, so he turned away and took a few more photos, focusing on a crown-like peak off to his right.

When he finished, he tried a few close-ups of some flowers, particularly the red paintbrush and the harebells. There were bearberries, too, and birds—so many birds. A grey one that reminded him of the whisky jack but wasn't quite the same. He bet Harper knew.

When he went back to the rock, she was leaned back on it, sunning herself. Even though he knew he shouldn't, he perched on the edge, leaned over and touched his lips to hers.

"Mmm," she hummed, and his blood raced. "Hello there."

"This is a nice piece of equipment."

"I assume you mean my camera," she said, opening one eye as she squinted against the sun.

"Oh, that, too," he replied, grinning.

She pushed up from the rock with a laugh. "You're incorrigible."

"So I've been told already today."

She laughed again. "Are you hungry? We can eat the picnic now if you want."

"I could eat."

He sat down next to her, but first took off her camera and handed it over. She put the cap on the lens and set it carefully beside her, then reached for the pack and the goodies inside. The first thing to emerge was a bottle of water. He uncapped it, took a drink and then handed it over to her.

Her throat bobbed as she swallowed, and then she licked her lips to catch any remaining moisture and he clenched his jaw. Tuesday night had whetted his appetite for her and now he couldn't stop thinking about holding her in his arms and kissing her. He didn't remember the last time a woman had held his thoughts captive quite so readily.

She handed the bottle back and then dug into the insulated pack. "What's in here?" she asked, digging around. She pulled out a package and peered at the label. "Hmm. Smoked turkey and gouda on light rye. Yours?"

He reached for it. "I'm guessing. I have no idea what's in there, so keep digging."

She took out a dish of crudités, and then another with a quinoa and chickpea salad—the vegetarian option—and finally strawberries, raspberries and plump blackberries with crème fraiche.

"Wow," she said, looking at the selections spread out over the rock. "This is amazing."

"I asked for a picnic and we got a feast." He had unwrapped his sandwich, but held it in his hand, forgotten, as he watched her take out a fork for her salad. She fluffed the grains a little bit, tasted and closed her eyes. "Oh, that's lovely."

She was lovely. And she appreciated everything. He loved that about her.

They ate for a while in silence, enjoying the view and the fine weather, a little cooler at the higher altitude but still perfectly comfortable. "It feels like we're picnicking on top of the world," he said, brushing off his hands and reaching for a baby carrot.

"Not quite. But close." She sighed, a happy, complete sound. "We are going to be able to hike a bit, yeah? Before they come back? There's a view from that ridge that I think is going to be spectacular."

"Do you feel up to that?"

"Yeah, I'm fine, particularly since I was saved the climb. Actually, the last few days I've felt great. Adele worries. She'd probably have a bird if she knew I was up here right now."

"She knows." He put down the crust of his bread and looked into her eyes. "I got a call from Dan last night."

"About this?" Her brows puckered above her nose.

"No, something else. But I mentioned today and he asked if I thought this was a good idea."

She hesitated for a moment before speaking again. "You didn't tell me that."

"I wasn't sure if I should. I don't want to make things more tense between you guys, you know?"

She nodded, looking down. "It's not even that it's particularly tense. I'm pregnant, not an invalid."

He laughed a little. "You certainly aren't." Then his smile slipped. "Dan accused me of trying to impress you."

She met his gaze. "Money doesn't impress me, Drew."

"Thank God. And I already knew that. Truly, I did this because I wanted to do something special and fun for you. Not to show off."

When she didn't answer, he reached out and touched her chin with his index finger, nudging a little so she'd look at him.

"What? Don't you think you're worth a little spoiling?"

She moved her head away from his finger and he knew he'd touched a nerve. "I'm sorry. I didn't mean to upset you."

"It's not that. It's more…oh, it's complicated."

"Then we don't have to talk about it now if you don't want." He let the matter go and reached for the dish of berries and the other of cream. He plucked out a raspberry, smeared it with some cream and offered it to her. "Peace offering?"

A smile flirted with her lips. "I can't resist berries."

"Or me?"

"Or you. And I'm scared for you to know it."

He popped the berry in her mouth. "I won't hurt you, Harper. And I'll be honest with you. Eyes wide open."

She chewed the berry and swallowed. "Like you were about being stinkin' rich?"

He laughed, and the sound carried over the valley. "Touché. I mean, when it comes to us. I won't lead you on or make promises I can't keep."

She avoided his eyes and selected another berry. "I appreciate that."

They packed up their picnic and shouldered their packs, ready to hike through the meadow to the peaks beyond before looping back again. The incline was only slightly challenging, and the views from the top were astounding. Drew took out his camera and took several pictures, and then watched as Harper worked her magic. She took her time, adjusting her position, working with her equipment, squinting at the light. When she was satisfied, she beckoned him over to where the faint trail met a junction. "This way is to the ridge," she said, pointing, and he looked at the incline. If she was up to it, he was totally game.

They went only maybe half a kilometer when she stopped, lifted her camera and fired off a quick few shots. "Look at that lake. Isn't it stunning? Now look at what's around it."

He squinted and looked, and she laughed. "Here." She held up her camera, though she kept it around her neck. "Look to the right of the lake, about halfway up, and use the zoom."

When he did, he saw a bull elk. "How did I miss that before?"

"It's a ways away, you know." He took a quick picture of the entire lake, and then adjusted to take one of the elk, always aware that they were tethered closely together by her camera strap. She smelled like something light and floral, fresh air, and the light sweat from hiking.

"Harper," he murmured, releasing the camera. He turned her toward him and cupped her face. "Damn," he whispered, and then kissed her. He wanted to do more, so much more, but knew it would be wrong. He was leaving and it would be unfair to her. But he wanted to, so much. She tasted like heaven and felt so alive in his arms. The camera dug into his diaphragm but he didn't care. This place was perfect, the day was perfect, and kissing her right now, with the Rockies all around them, was the most natural and important thing in the world.

She sighed against his lips as the kiss eased. "Oh, Drew. What are we doing?"

"I don't know. I just know it feels good."

She nodded. "Me, too. When you kiss me…"

She broke off, took a deep, wobbly breath.

"What, Harper? What happens when I kiss you?"

"I forget about everything. There's only you and me and all the things you make me feel. I know it's not wise but I can't seem to help myself."

"That's a dangerous thing to say to a man like me."

She looked up at him then, her blue eyes wide and full of wonder. "No, it's not. Because I trust you." She smiled a little. "You said you would never lie to me."

He swallowed tightly and put an inch or two between them. When it came to relationships he wasn't reliable, and the last thing he wanted to do was hurt Harper. She was too special. He knew what a broken heart looked like and he didn't want to be responsible for that again.

"You shouldn't trust me," he replied, his voice rough. "I'm good in business, Harper, but I suck at romance. Lies or not." He remembered the accusations leveled at him over the last few years. Commitment-phobe. Married to his work. "My top focus is Aspen Outfitters. That's not going to change."

"I know." She lifted her hand and ran her fingers over his jawline. "But I also know I trust you because you've been honest about that from the beginning. I'm not asking for more than you're offering, Drew."

But that was the problem. As he kissed her again, he knew he wanted to offer her more than he should. And to do so would only lead to hurt all around.

Maybe Dan was right. Maybe he didn't know what he was doing.

CHAPTER TEN

THEY MADE THEIR way back toward the crest where they'd be picked up again, and Harper paused to catch her breath. There was more going on in her mind and body than simple physical exertion. Right now she was simply full of Drew. The way he looked and felt and tasted. What he'd said and the husky sound of his voice...she was in huge danger of falling for him. There was so much more than charm and charisma. There was a good, strong man beneath that persona. A man who freely admitted that work came before personal relationships, so why couldn't she seem to stay away?

Instead they came to an uneven bit of ground, and Drew held out his hand. She took it, loving the feel of her palm against his.

And when she was over the rocks, she kept her fingers entwined with his. Days. They had only days left to enjoy each other. Why shouldn't they?

She looked over at him and he sensed her gaze and looked back, a smile on his face. Harper felt something expand in her chest that was new and exciting. She rather thought it might be happiness. Did she dare hold on to it, even for a brief time? Her whole life she'd held herself apart from relationships, always afraid of getting hurt when they ended. Until she moved here, and she made a best friend—Adele. For the first time, she was confident that despite any awkwardness now, she and Adele would still be best friends and they'd work their way through the current dynamic.

She wasn't afraid to care for Drew right now. She had no unrealistic expectations. Maybe it was time to live for the moment. Take chances, and live life with a bit of messiness. It had to be better than always being the one behind the lens, watching life happen to other people. She was so tired of being on the outside, even if she'd been the one to put herself there. The revelation was amazingly liberating.

"You're awfully quiet," Drew said, tugging on her hand.

"Walking is good for thinking, and thinking is good for working out problems."

"Do you have problems to be worked out?" They made it to the crest and she leaned back, stretching with her hands on her hips.

"A few. It's more realizations, I guess." Her pulse quickened, a little nervous about what she was going to say. "I think I've spent a good portion of my life avoiding risks. But it's not really living, you know?"

He squeezed her fingers. "Hiding behind your lens?"

She laughed a little. "Maybe. And I got comfortable there. Never letting myself get too close to people because I knew eventually I'd have to say goodbye. But I can't seem to do that with you. I know you're leaving soon. I know this will go nowhere after next week. But if I shut this down…" She caught her breath. "If I shut this down, what's between us, I know I'm going to regret it."

He stared at her for a long moment. "What do you want, Harper?"

Courage began to blossom in her chest, even as the faint sound of helicopter rotors started to pulse through the air. "I want to live. I want to stop playing it safe all of the time. I want to get out of my comfort zone now and again and do something daring."

"You don't call what you're doing for Adele and Dan daring?" Drew lifted an eyebrow.

"Yes and no. I mean, I'm really pregnant. But when this is over, the whole plan is to go back to my safe and boring life. At first that was all I really wanted, but what if that's not enough anymore? What if I want…helicopter rides through the mountains? Kisses on my porch? Surprises?"

The sound grew louder and she knew she had

to get this out before the pilot landed. "The last few weeks, seeing you…it's been good for me. I can feel it. I've been so afraid of getting hurt, but I think what's always made me so cautious is being blindsided."

"What do you mean?"

"I mean, every time I moved, it came out of the blue. My dad would get a change of orders and we'd move. New base, new town, new schools. New teachers, new kids who always stared at the new girl in class. For the first few times, I made good friends, but then it hurt so much to move again and say goodbye. Once I hit nine or ten, I stopped making friends. I understood that I'd have to leave again. By the time I was twelve, I had my first camera, and it became my friend. It never got left behind."

Drew let out a breath. "Jeez, Harper. That sounds so lonely. I was really lucky to have my brother and sisters, you know? And we lived in the same house growing up." He shook his head. "Man. You were lonely and I felt claustrophobic. I love my family, but I couldn't wait to get out on my own. The last thing I wanted was to be stuck in one place."

She squeezed his fingers. "I'm not blindsided this time. Like you said, eyes open." The chopper got closer and the wind started to whip her hair as she raised her voice to be heard. "I'm ready for an adventure, Drew!"

His only answer was a quicksilver smile as the chopper hovered, inching its way toward the bluff. He held her hand tightly as they moved to the helicopter. And when they were buckled up and the chopper lifted off and then dropped over the side to skim down the valley, Harper kept her eyes open and went along for the ride.

Drew put his pack in the back of the car and took a deep breath. He had no idea what to do next. His feelings for Harper were complicated, but he'd felt in control of them. Or at least in control of how the next week would play out. Maybe seeing each other a few more times, enjoying each other's company and a mutual goodbye at the end with no hard feelings.

Today had changed all that.

She hadn't said anything since they'd disembarked. They had maybe fifteen minutes in the car to decide what would happen next. And he knew what he wanted to happen and what should happen.

He should drop her off and go back to the hotel. And yet, he wasn't ready for the day to be over. Harper deserved to be treated like the special woman she was, and he wanted to be the man to do it.

Neither said anything until they got close to the townsite exit. Then Drew looked over at her. "I don't want today to end. Come back to the hotel for dinner."

He had to turn his attention back to the road but he felt her gaze on his face. "To dinner?"

He nodded, glancing over again. "I can take you home to change. It's been too wonderful a day for it to end now."

She sighed. "We could always order a pizza. You don't need to go to all this trouble."

"I want to," he insisted. They slowed for a group of tourists crossing the street. "It's not trouble, Harper. It's a pleasure. I want to spend more time with you. And I want to…to show you that you're special."

"At your hotel."

He understood what she was and wasn't saying. "Yes, at my hotel. But it doesn't have to be there. I don't want to pressure you into anything."

There was a pause of perhaps two seconds, and then she answered, "The Cascade sounds fine."

And with that admission, the air snapped with electricity and the anticipation of what was to come. What did he do? Charm her over dinner? Drive her home again as soon as the meal was over? Wait for her to make a move? He felt as unsure as a teenager faced with undoing a girl's bra for the first time. One wrong move and it would be all over. Maybe he should just play it cool.

He parked in her narrow driveway and she unbuckled her seat belt. Drew reached over and took her hand before she could take the keys out of the ignition.

"I'm not sure what to say or do right now," he admitted. "This is nerve-racking as hell."

She blew out a breath. "For me, too. But first I have to change into something more appropriate. Do you mind if I have a quick shower?" She pulled her hand away and opened her door.

It helped that she was also nervous. Or maybe it didn't...perhaps one of them being tied up in knots was more than enough. Regardless, he followed her lead and got out of the car, then grabbed both their packs while she got her camera bag. He tried to block out the idea of her under the hot shower spray and instead on the evening ahead...which was nearly as bad.

The day had been warm, but the wind took on a sudden chill as the sun went under a cloud. Drew looked up, surprised to see a wall of clouds closing in.

Once inside the house, Drew put down the backpacks and reached for Harper's hand. "Can I kiss you?"

She blushed prettily, the colour highlighting the freckles on her nose as she nodded. He stepped forward and kissed her, a soft, gentle hello of a kiss that reached in and grabbed him right by the heart with its hesitancy and sweetness.

Leaving her was going to be harder than she knew.

He broke off the kiss. "Go have your shower. I'm starving."

"I won't be long. There are drinks in the fridge if you want one."

He got himself a can of ginger ale and settled in the living room on the sofa while the water ran for the shower. How was this evening really going to play out? There was no question he wanted to kiss her again. But how far did he want to go?

His brother's words rang in his ears: *I hope you know what you're doing.*

He didn't. Not even close.

She came back out a few minutes later, her hair wet and darker than usual, which made her pale skin and blue eyes stand out. She wore a light, floral maxi dress that accentuated her breasts but fell in soft folds to the floor, where her toes peeked out from little sandals. She came to sit beside him and that floral scent that had only been hinted at earlier now filled the air around him. Her shampoo, he realized. Whatever it was, it made his blood stir.

"Feel better?" he asked.

"Much." She smiled softly. "Are you ready?"

"I am if you are."

She got up and put her hand on her lower back.

He rose and reached over, touching the muscles just above her sacrum. "Is your back bothering you?"

"A little. The doctor said it might bother me a bit because my body is changing and tendons and stuff." She laughed a bit, but he stood behind her and used his thumbs to rub on the spot where she'd pressed her hand. Over the years he'd come to rely on a massage therapist a lot to deal with aches and pains after difficult expeditions.

"Oh my God, that feels good," she said, her voice almost a moan as she relaxed beneath his fingertips.

He tried not to react to her words. It was difficult, because the attraction was insane, and having his hands on her was arousing, plain and simple. But this wasn't the moment. This was a time for being caring and helpful. As he massaged a tight muscle, the first rumblings of thunder began.

"Have you tried yoga? Like, a prenatal kind or something? It might help with any stiffness or lower back issues."

"I haven't. I've been so busy that my exercise routine has been walking and getting out for the odd hike."

His thumbs rubbed in concentric circles. "Well, maybe you can look into it. Or go for prenatal massage."

"If it's anything like you're doing right now, that's a brilliant idea," she murmured. "That feels amazing."

You have no idea, he thought, but instead he

worked on the tight muscles that she probably over-used today in addition to the changes happening inside her body.

Lightning flashed outside the window, followed by a deeper rumble of thunder a few seconds later. "Looks like we're in for some rain," he mused.

"I'm glad we're not in the chopper now." She gasped a little as he touched a particularly tight area.

"Me, too."

After a few minutes she straightened. "Thanks, Drew," she said, and despite the "normal" tone to her voice, there was a huskiness underlying it that lent an intimacy to the moment. "I think that's good."

Maybe, but touching her had been a mistake. He didn't want to stop. Maybe not ever.

Harper grabbed her purse and Drew reached into his pocket for the keys. He didn't know how the evening would end, but as long as he was with Harper, it was bound to be perfect.

Harper chose to wait in the lounge while Drew cleaned up. Being in his hotel room might be a little too dangerous. She was up for an adventure, but not looking to be totally reckless. Drew was a particularly potent temptation she wasn't sure she could resist.

She was halfway through a glass of sparkling

water when Drew reappeared, and she caught her breath.

He hadn't been more than fifteen minutes, but he'd showered and changed into dress pants and a blue shirt, open at the collar but pressed and expensive looking. That women turned their heads to watch him didn't escape her attention, and she smiled up at him as he approached. He was so handsome. And his smile…it warmed her from the inside out, like it was just for her.

"What a transformation," she said, turning to him. "And fast."

"I told you that happens when I'm properly motivated."

They were led to their table in the corner, looking out over the townsite and valley below. At one end of the view, the sun was still shining, but at the other, storm clouds rolled in, dark grey and ominous. As she watched, a flash of lightning forked down from a black cloud. "We're in for some weather," she observed, and the electricity of the storm mirrored the excitement inside her. Today had marked a turning point and it left her feeling off balance but also exhilarated.

"Would you like another sparkling water? A virgin cocktail?"

She turned from the view, scanned the drink menu and looked up at the waiter. "Could I get a Paloma Fizz, no tequila?"

"Of course. And you, sir?"

He ordered a whiskey, neat, and the waiter slipped away.

"Drew, this is lovely. Truly."

"I'm glad. Much better than take-out pizza, don't you think?"

She laughed lightly. "Pizza has its place," she replied, fiddling with her napkin. "But you're right. There's something about being here...the hotel is one of my favorites. The steps and railings are practically works of art." She looked down and softened her voice. "You're spoiling me today."

The waiter returned with their drinks and she took a sip of the rosemary-infused grapefruit soda. The sparkles sat on her tongue for a moment and she sighed, enjoying the setting and the company. Maybe she wasn't high maintenance, but it was nice feeling special and pampered now and again. She looked over at Drew and the curl of attraction wound through her again.

"What?" he asked.

Her cheeks heated. "Nothing." She focused on her menu but felt his gaze on her as she perused the selections. The light through the windows darkened from the storm clouds, and a young man clad in black came around with a lighter and lit the candles on the table. Thunder rumbled outside, a low growl that made Harper glad they weren't outside any longer.

They ordered and the appetizers were served quickly and discreetly. She took one bite of the watercress and endive salad and sighed with happiness at the fruity sharpness of the fig dressing. Drew indulged in escargot, and then they dined on risotto primavera and lobster carbonara. Rain spattered on the windows but then the storm moved off, onward through the valley and toward the foothills.

She was starting to get full when she asked what she'd been wondering all day. "Did you really say Aspen made thirty million last year? Three-zero?"

He nodded. "Yeah. Up from twenty-six and change the year before. We've been seeing steady growth. We also do a profit share with our employees, so twice a year they get an extra deposit into their account. I keep them happy, they keep me in business."

"I really didn't have any idea. Neither Dan or Adele said anything."

"Does it matter?" He took a sip of ice water and watched her steadily.

That question was easy to answer. "No. It doesn't make you any more likable...or unlikable, either." She gave a sideways grin. "I'm just...wow. You really are driven, aren't you?"

He shrugged. "Like I said the other day. Work hard, play hard. Now I have a question for you."

"Sure."

"If you'd known I was a millionaire, would your answer at the wedding have been different?"

She started to laugh, and dabbed her lips with her napkin. She wasn't insulted in the least. "Do I look like the type who would see dollar signs?"

He chuckled, too. "No, but I kind of hoped you were. Because then I wouldn't have taken it so personally."

She lifted an eyebrow. "I'd feel bad, if I thought you really meant that."

His grin grew. "I like how you challenge me, Harper. I like it a lot."

Money really didn't turn her head, but she had to admit that she did see him differently now. Not better, not worse, but just different. He was a millionaire at age twenty-eight with a chain of his own stores. It was difficult not to respect that. It also widened the gap between them significantly. There were months she could barely pay the rent.

But none of that really mattered when they were together. Sure, days like today didn't make him bat an eye, but deep down, Drew was the guy who'd talked to a bighorn sheep and enjoyed a cone of ice cream on a busy street. The one who rubbed her ankle while she slept on a porch swing. Who made her laugh without trying, and made her toes curl when he kissed her.

They ordered dessert—Earl Grey panna cotta for her and chestnut tiramisu for him, and she let the flavors sit on her tongue. "I've never had something like this in my life," she sighed happily. "Today has been…oh, Drew. It's been like a fairy tale. And tomorrow I get to go back to my humdrum life."

It also appeared the storms weren't over. A new front rolled down through the mountains, a wall of foreboding cloud that brought with it unsettling wind and flashes of lightning. Thunder growled and then boomed, close enough that she jumped when it rattled the crystal on the table.

"You should see your eyes," he said, smiling a little.

"I'm very glad we're safe and sound inside." The lights flickered but stayed on. "And you didn't even flinch."

"I love thunderstorms." At her raised eyebrow, he laughed. "We're really different in some ways, aren't we?" He reached over and took her hand. "I know you moved around a lot as a kid. That you had a hard time making friends and establishing relationships. But there's more, isn't there? Something that holds you back."

"Why do you say that?"

"Because it's not friends you shy away from. It's intimacy. Someone hurt you." His gaze locked with hers. "I know because you have the same look in your eyes as someone else did once, when I broke their heart."

The rest of her dessert was forgotten. Whether he'd initiated the breakup or not, he hadn't come out of it unscathed.

And for the first time, she spoke about Jared.

"The truth is, I did meet someone once, and it was one of those crazy whirlwind-attraction deals. I fell like a ton of bricks at the ripe old age of twenty-two. He was hot and funny and sexy and I was really swept away, thinking he could be The One. He proposed, and I was thrilled. We were going to elope and just be crazy. Instead, he broke off the engagement and disappeared. I was heartbroken—and blindsided yet again. Oddly enough, that was when my photography really started to take off."

"Because you kept hiding."

"And damn, but I was good at it."

His thumb traced circles over her hand, and she blinked back a little moisture that had gathered in the corners of her eyes. "I feel so foolish now. But then…it was as if no one thought I was worth hanging around for."

"So what changed?"

"Adele. She's the best friend I've ever had. I've made a life for myself here. I put down the roots I've never really had before, but I'm still not totally happy. I've been so busy trying to protect my life I stopped really living it. I want to start living again, even if it's just for a few weeks." She held his gaze and took a breath. "With you."

The lights flickered again, but his thumb kept circling, the pressure warm and soothing. "As long as you know that I can't stay. That the plan hasn't changed." The smile had slid off his face, and he was as serious as she'd ever seen him.

"Oh, I know that. I'm just tired of denying myself things that make me happy because they might not last forever. That not living, that's pure avoidance."

She turned her hand over and linked her fingers with his. "I'm going to miss you when you're gone. But I want to look back on this time as a happy memory, not another case of me choosing the safe route and missing out."

She'd never considered Drew the kind of man to blush, but right now heat was creeping up his neck and into his cheeks. "Then don't leave yet. When we finish dinner…come back to my room. The night doesn't have to end."

"We don't exactly have time to waste, do we?" Her words came out breathy, as if she'd been walking too fast.

He let out a big breath. "I don't… I just…" His eyes were wide and serious. "Despite what you may think of me, this isn't something I take lightly. Or casually."

"I'm glad." Nerves bubbled, both from anticipation and from anxiety. This was all new territory.

Moments later Drew signed the slip charging

the meal to his room, and then held out his hand. "Shall we?" he asked.

She put her hand in his again and let him lead her out of the restaurant. They were going to his hotel room. She wasn't sure what she wanted to happen, but she knew something was going to. She wanted it to.

They rode up the elevator in silence, nervousness flooding her from head to toe. Her sandals made slapping sounds on the hall carpet until they reached his door and he waved his key card over the sensor.

His suite was gorgeous. She'd been in Cascade rooms before, doing before-the-wedding photos and the like, but she'd never been in this one. A massive sitting area was flanked by a dining table and chairs. Off to the left was the bedroom, and she took a few steps toward it, as if drawn by a magnet. The king-size bed was the centerpiece, covered with a fluffy gold duvet. Throw pillows in jewel tones were placed strategically on the bed. The view from the window was staggering in its beauty.

She was here. In his hotel room. The Presidential Suite, wasn't it?

The door shut with a quiet click, and then he was there behind her, his hands on her shoulders as he leaned forward and kissed her hair.

Her entire body went into high alert. When a

man like Drew Brimicombe put his full attention on a woman, it was an intoxicating feeling.

"Hi," she said, knowing it sounded stupid, unsure of what else to say.

"Hi." His breath was warm on her neck and goose bumps broke out over her skin. "How are you?"

She bit down on her lip. "Nervous. Afraid of doing the wrong thing."

He turned her to face him. "Nothing you say or do will be the wrong thing."

"Really?" She ran her hands over the soft fabric of her skirt. "I'm pretty sure I can be an idiot very easily. Like today, when you told me you were rich. I felt pretty stupid. This is the Presidential Suite, isn't it?"

That sexy grin crawled up his cheek once more. "I told you I was able to snag a cancellation. It was the only room available."

She shook her head but laughed a little. This whole thing was surreal.

He took her fingers in his. "Harper, I just want you to know that tonight is entirely up to you and what you want. You're in control."

When he said it, she realized exactly how much she'd felt out of control the last few months. Once she'd taken the pregnancy test, her life hadn't really been her own. But this decision was, and it felt good.

Her heart pounded so hard she could feel it against her ribs. Her breath shortened; she had never been one to take the lead in sexual situations. But this time he was waiting, leaving it up to her, giving her complete autonomy. It was a dizzying thought. She reached out and put her hand against his chest, touching him but still keeping him a few inches away. Her heart pounded, from excitement but also fear. "I do want this," she said on a breath. "So much it hurts."

"Then tell me." His thumbs were hooked in his front pockets, and she saw them close tighter over the fabric. "Show me."

She stood on tiptoe and kissed him, softly, slowly, as if they had all the time in the world. When she'd tasted her fill—for the time being—she stood back away from him.

And knew this wasn't the right time, or the right place. She was so close to giving her heart away. If they made love, it would only make things worse. She knew he was leaving. But she was conveniently ignoring the depth of her feelings. Right now, looking up at him, she was perilously close to losing herself.

"It's not the right time, is it?" he asked, as if reading her thoughts.

She shook her head.

He took a big breath and then let it out. "Then let's just hang out. Watch a movie and raid the mini bar for snacks."

Relief flooded through her. "Oh, I've always wanted to do that!"

He laughed, and squeezed her hand. "I just want to spend time with you. In bed, out of it…it doesn't matter. Look at the pay-per-view and pick something out." He gave her a stern look. "No porn. I'm already going to need a few minutes to, uh…"

She burst out laughing. Oh, she could love him so very easily. He was sexy and kind and made her smile all the time.

And when they started the movie and she lay on the bed curled up in his arms, it was the best feeling in the world.

When Harper woke, it was twilight.

She carefully rolled to her side and watched him sleep, his lips slightly parted and his eyelashes on the crests of his cheeks. They were on top of the covers, and the TV was shut off. She must have fallen asleep first. She didn't remember watching the end of the movie. It had been so cozy in Drew's arms.

It had been a perfect day, better than any she could ever remember. Her heart caught. She couldn't fall in love with him. She'd promised herself she wouldn't. And yet now, watching him sleep, there was an expansive feeling in her chest that told her she was dangerously close to losing her heart.

To the one man who didn't want it. Who wasn't looking for love. *It's okay*, she told herself. *I knew all along he was going. I'm going to cherish this time as a special memory.*

The problem was, she was starting to feel as if she didn't want just memories. She wanted *him*.

A funny sound reached her ears, some sort of music. She blinked and realized it was her phone, which she'd left in her purse. It stopped ringing, but then started again, and with a sigh she slid off the bed and tiptoed out to the living room to grab it.

The display showed Adele's number. She kept her voice low so she hopefully wouldn't wake Drew.

"Hello, Adele."

"Oh, good, you're there. I've been worried sick."

"You have? I didn't answer the first time you called because I was sleeping."

It wasn't exactly a lie.

"But I texted you like ten times."

"Sorry. It was a long nap."

Adele let out a long breath. "Okay. I'm sorry. I knew you'd gone into the mountains today and then the storm blew in and the power went out and I was so worried."

Yes, because clearly she couldn't be trusted to take care of herself. Irritation flared, an emotion that felt out of place. Usually she was so easygoing. What had happened to change that? It couldn't be Adele's hovering; Harper knew her friend was just concerned. There was a lot at stake.

Maybe it was stress. Hormones. Or the fact that Drew's arrival had suddenly made her unsettled and longing for…more.

"I'm fine," she said, as kindly as she could muster. "We went early this morning and were back by late afternoon, before the storm blew in. No worries at all. I got some great pictures and it was good to be outdoors for the day. I needed it."

"And you didn't overdo it?"

Harper pinched her nose, willing herself to be patient. "No, I didn't. We took our time and rested lots. Had a picnic in the meadow at the top. I'm fine. The baby's fine."

Adele's exhale sounded relieved. "And we're still going to do lunch next week?"

Drew called her name and she went to the door of the bedroom, putting a finger to her lips as she met his gaze. "How about Tuesday?" she asked Adele. "Monday I'll be trying to catch up after this week's wedding."

"Tuesday's fine. I miss seeing you, Harper. You haven't even been here for dinner in ages. Not since we had our last appointment."

"I know. You know what summer is like. Busiest time of year."

"You know it." The conversation turned to

wedding discussion and Harper rolled her eyes at
Drew, eliciting a snort from him. When Adele had
finally finished with her story, Harper interjected.

"Adele, I'm still really tired. I'm going to go
back to bed. I don't mean to cut this off…" She
wondered if her nose would grow like Pinocchio's
for lying. But if she said she was in Drew's hotel
room, Adele would lose her mind.

"Oh! Of course. I'll text you about Tuesday. And
glad you're okay. Stay dry. I'm glad the power's
back on."

That was news to Harper, and she let out a
breath. "Me, too."

"Oh, one more thing. How was Drew today?"

Funny how she added it on at the very end, as
an afterthought. Harper had no doubt that Adele's
first priority was making sure Harper was home
and okay, but she also knew that Adele would be
dying to know about her outing with Drew.

"Oh, fine. I'm sure Dan told you he hired a helicopter. I braved it, even with my fear of heights.
So I didn't even have to hike that far." She rolled
her eyes at Drew again, and his brown eyes lit up
with mischief. "I'll tell you all about it at lunch."

"Okay. Well…talk soon."

Harper hung up and went to sit on the edge of
the bed. "Adele was worried. But apparently the
power is back on."

He nodded. "You fell asleep. I didn't have the

heart to wake you. Then you took me with you." His smile was adorable.

Then he leaned up on an elbow and kissed her, just a simple, sweet kiss, but it caught her by surprise. Then he pulled back, lifted her hand and kissed it. Despite all her best intentions, Harper felt herself make the remaining slide straight into love.

CHAPTER ELEVEN

DREW HELD HARPER'S hand in his and tried not to show that inside he was freaking out.

It wasn't that he wanted her to leave, or that their time together had been a mistake. He was freaking out because for the first time in his life, he wanted to stay somewhere and never leave.

With her.

Her eyes sparkled at him with good humor. There was nothing he wanted more than for her to spend the rest of the night right here, in his bed.

But she couldn't. The very idea made his insides freeze with fear. Instead he looked into her eyes, lifted her hand and kissed her fingers.

He was falling in love. At least that's what he figured it was, because it was unlike any other feeling he'd experienced. It should be impossible to feel terrified and happy all at once. Right now terrified was tangling with desire and he had no idea what to do about it.

"I should probably get going," she said softly, and there was a pause. Was she waiting for him to ask her to stay?

He wanted to. God, did he want to. But he knew it was better for everyone if he didn't. "I suppose you have work in the morning."

"Yeah, and a wedding rehearsal tomorrow night." But her easy words didn't reach her eyes. It wasn't how he wanted their date to end, but sex was out of the question. It wouldn't be fair to either of them. Besides, she had enough complications with the pregnancy in the months ahead.

It had nothing to do with being afraid. Nothing.

"Harper, about earlier… I want you to know that I think we made the right decision. I want to be with you. It's just that if we go all in with this, it's going to make it harder next Friday when I fly out."

She nodded a tiny bit. "Next Friday, then. That's the day?"

"I've got a flight early afternoon, through LA."

"You didn't mention it before."

"It happened yesterday. And today I forgot about it while we were out."

Which wasn't exactly true. He'd remembered but hadn't seen the need to bring it into the conversation. Now it seemed important. To set boundaries where a few hours ago there'd been none.

She didn't say anything, and her thumb stopped moving on his hand. The knot of panic doubled in size.

"Listen," he said softly, pulling his hand away

and brushing hair away from her face. "We both know where this is going and where it isn't. I don't want to hurt you, Harper. And I don't want to make false promises." The knot started to actually hurt now. "You told me about the guy you fell for and how much it hurt when he left. I don't want to be that guy. I've been that man before and the last thing I want to do is hurt you."

"You've been honest from the beginning and so have I. I know you're not a forever kind of guy, Drew. I've got my eyes wide open, remember?"

She didn't mean the words as an accusation, so why did it feel that way?

"I know you do. But…and I can't believe I'm about to say this…it might be good for us to use a little bit of caution, at least." He wanted to kiss her so badly right now he ached with it. She looked so soft, so vulnerable, and yet determined, too. He loved that about her.

Love. Exactly the reason he had to go.

She grinned. "I'm already pregnant. We don't have to worry too much about caution."

He closed his eyes, trying not to smile at her dry crack at humor. "You're deliberately misunderstanding me, and that's okay." He opened his eyes again. In the dim light through the blinds her eyes seemed dark and grey and her freckles were barely noticeable. He wished he was as adept with a camera as she was. She'd make a stunning photo right now. "I'm going to be back in town now and again, Harper. For the store. To see Dan. I don't want it to be awkward or worse, tense and angry between us. Does that make sense?"

"Yes," she breathed, and she blinked a few times. He didn't see tears, thank God. If she cried he wouldn't be able to handle it. "You're protecting yourself."

"And you." It was true. Sure, he was panicked enough for both of them, but he also didn't want to hurt her. "When I go, I want it to be with you smiling. If we play house for the next week, I'm not sure either of us will be able to keep our perspective."

Her eyes flashed. "Then I'll go right now, and we'll let that be it. The perfect ending to a perfect day."

It was like a punch to the gut, but he answered calmly, "If that's what you want."

Silence dropped over the room.

She touched his shoulder. "I'm sorry I snapped," she murmured. "It's just that you make me feel…" Her cheeks flamed. "Ugh, this is so hard."

"I make you feel what?"

"Desirable. Wanted. I haven't felt that way in a very long time. You can't expect me to give it up after an hour." She was bright red now. "I sound like a desperate idiot."

"No, you don't. And I'm glad. Because you are

wanted. And very, very desirable. That's what makes this so hard. I'm trying to do the right thing."

He got up from the bed and reached for his shoes. "Come on. I'll take you home. And we'll both respect each other in the morning."

She laughed a little, and it put his mind at ease.

But when he kissed her goodbye at her door, his heart caught. He was in far deeper than he intended. And he wasn't sure he had it in him to stay away.

Harper didn't see Drew at all on Friday, and she spent the evening at the rehearsal for Saturday's wedding. Saturday she woke early and showered, dressing in a comfortable maxi dress for the day. Some of her more fitted clothing was getting too tight around the middle now as her waist thickened. In another month she'd really be starting to show. She put her hand to her belly and thought about the baby growing there. She hadn't even felt him or her move yet. Sometimes it was hard to believe there was really a baby in there.

At nine there was a knock on the door. She was putting makeup on and had eye shadow on only one eye when she went to answer. It was Drew, carrying a paper bag and holding a tray with cups.

"I brought breakfast," he announced, then stepped inside and gave her a kiss.

"Oh! You didn't need to do that."

"I know. But I missed seeing you yesterday, and you have the wedding all day today, so I thought this might be my window of opportunity. I went out for a morning walk and ended up here."

He looked delicious, as usual. Just jeans and a T-shirt but the way they fit his lean body made her mouth water.

And she did have to eat. Now that the sickness was gone, breakfast was no longer a challenge. She craved it.

"I haven't eaten, so thanks."

"Uh, you're lopsided." He pointed to her face.

"Oh! I was putting on makeup when you knocked. Make yourself at home and I'll do the other eye." She grinned at him and already her heart felt lighter as she faced the day. She hadn't been quite sure how they'd left things Thursday night, but he seemed his old self. If breakfast was all she got of Drew today, she'd take it. In a heartbeat.

She didn't normally wear a lot of makeup, so it took no time at all for her to brush on her eye shadow, add a tiny bit of eyeliner and a swipe of mascara on her lashes. She went back to the kitchen with matching eyes and found Drew putting breakfast on plates.

"Egg and cheese on sourdough for you, and bacon, egg and cheese on a biscuit for me. And fruit salad."

Eggs. She craved them all the time now. Maybe her body needed the protein. Stomach growling, she sat at the table and reached for her fork, spearing a piece of melon.

"This is beyond nice. And it'll fuel me through the morning, too, until I have time to grab a protein bar or something. I have to grab snacks on the run during the day until the reception, when I can gobble a meal quickly." She took a bite of sandwich, chewed and swallowed. "Juny's started coming with me, too, as my assistant. I'm letting her do more and more. She has a good eye and she can help more when I get closer to the due date."

"Plus it takes some of the pressure off you."

"I'll confess, the last few weddings have been long and I've gotten really tired. It's been nice to have someone help set up and lug stuff from the car rather doing it all alone." She shrugged. "I can do it, but it's nice to work as a team. Sometimes it seems as if I need to be in two places at once."

"Well, you look pretty."

She nudged him. "Thank you, though compliments aren't necessary."

"It's the truth. You always look pretty. Though Dan and Adele's wedding was something else. You looked…" He paused as he searched for the right words. "Like a classic movie star." He took the lid off her tea and slid it across the table to her. "So, was it as hard saying no to me as it is for me to say no to you?"

She met his gaze. "Is it hard to say no to me, Drew?" She held her breath, waiting for his answer.

"More than you can imagine."

Her heart expanded. She was glad. It made her feel as if she mattered. That despite her efforts to hide, someone actually saw past the barriers she put up and saw her.

"Then no, it wasn't as hard for me."

He burst out laughing. "Cheeky."

She joined in the laughter. "Naw, not really. It's just that the guy at the wedding? That wasn't the real Drew. Not really. I like you better now."

His gaze warmed. "I like you, too, Harper."

They were still staring at each other when her phone rang. She reached inside her bag and pulled it out. "It's Juny."

Two minutes later she hung up, turning her worried gaze to Drew. "Juny's girlfriend, Renée, was in an accident. She's okay, or at least she's going to be okay, but they're transporting her to Calgary to the Foothills Hospital."

"Oh, no." Drew's face wrinkled in concern. "Does Juny need anything? Is she all right?"

"She's fine. She wasn't in the car, but she's going to the hospital to be with Renée."

"Of course. What happened?"

"Juny doesn't quite know. I wish I could go with her, but I've got the wedding."

"And she was supposed to be helping you today."

"I can manage alone. I do it all the time." There was no question of expecting Juny to come to work. Not with something like this. It would be a long day, but she could rest tomorrow.

"I could help you."

She'd picked up her tea, but paused before taking a drink. "You?" She chuckled. "I know I let you use my camera yesterday, but Drew."

"Ha, ha," he replied, but he persisted. "I mean, I can carry your stuff for you. Be your right hand. You need a drink or food or anything, I can help. You were planning on having extra hands today. I'm certainly not as qualified as Juny, but I can take orders."

She was touched by his offer. "You? Take orders? Mr. President and CEO?"

"Yeah, me. Unless you'd rather I not be in your professional space. I understand that."

The idea of him being with her on a job didn't bother her in the least. "No, it's not that. But you'll be bored, won't you?"

"Maybe. Maybe not."

And having someone along to do the heavy lifting did sound wonderful. "Okay, but only if you have something suitable to wear."

"If you'll run me to the hotel, I can be ready in fifteen minutes."

After Thursday night's quick change, she didn't doubt him. "Done."

"Then it's settled. Now eat, and we'll get this show on the road."

They loaded all her equipment in the car and by ten thirty they were on the way to the Cascade for Drew to change. He was back in the promised fifteen minutes, and then it was off to the bride's home in Canmore. Harper looked over at Drew, sitting so calmly in her passenger seat yet again. What was she thinking, letting him come along? It was impossible to pretend that her feelings were anything other than love. She loved him. Was in love with him. Would have taken the whole week to be with him—in all ways—and dealt with the heartbreak at the end. Maybe that was what scared her the most. She wasn't used to such a lack of emotional caution. That Drew was the one being reasonable and thinking long term was a total flip of what she figured was their usual roles.

And it wasn't like he would never be back to Banff again, was it? His store would be here. Dan was here. Just because she'd fallen in love with him didn't mean they had to rush everything.

"Penny for your thoughts," he said, his gaze on her profile.

"We don't have pennies anymore in Canada," she replied. "Remember?"

"Right. Okay, I'll round up. Nickel for your thoughts."

She chuckled and realized how much she'd laughed since he'd arrived in Banff. "You make me laugh, you know that? It's nice."

"Is that what you were thinking?"

"No."

"Do I want to know?"

"I was thinking how nice you look in that colour blue." His shirt was the same colour as the open sky. Now that they were traveling east, the peaks were beside and behind them, with the rolling foothills giving way to a pristine blue without a cloud to mar it.

"It's okay I didn't wear a tie?"

Drew wasn't a tie kind of man. He was the kind who dressed up and then undid a few buttons for a more relaxed look. She loved it. "It's fine."

"So where's this wedding?"

"First we go to the bride's home and take some pictures of her and the bridesmaids and her mom, that kind of thing. Then it's off to the church. We'll get some photos of the groom and his groomsmen there, as they wait in a room behind the sanctuary. I'll set up and take some congregational shots, and then when the bride arrives it's really game on."

She looked over. "Once we get to the church, it

all happens rather quickly and with precise timing. If you're there with my bag, it'll help a lot." She smiled. "I even tucked a smaller camera in there for you. I thought you might like to have some fun and take some pictures of your own."

He gaped at her. "Are you serious? I can barely handle my little digital one."

"Yeah, but sometimes there's a candid that turns out great, or that I can edit a bit. You don't have to take any if you don't want to. I know this is my thing and you're not required to get excited about it. But it's there if you want it."

"I'll see. It might be fun."

They arrived at the bride's house, and Harper quickly rounded up the women of the wedding party and organized some shots while Drew got two of the bags from the car. They spent an hour there, getting pictures of the dress on the hanger, the flowers, the bride's mother adjusting her veil, the engagement ring and several of the bridesmaids and bride together. When the posed pictures were done, Drew gathered up most of the gear while Harper snapped candids of the family and friends present. There was one of the bride laughing with her father, and another of the flower girl showing an aunt her new white shoes. Those were the kind of memory photos she loved best.

At one fifteen she let the bride know they were heading for the church.

Set right on Main Street, the church was small
and quaint with a white picket fence out front. It
was the first time Harper had done a wedding here,
and despite the simplicity of it, she knew it would
be a favorite. There was something solid and reassuring about the old-fashioned wooden pews and
the sturdy pulpit at the front. A slightly faded red
carpet led the way up the aisle. The pews sported
white tulle bows and flowers as pew markers. She
stopped at the top of the aisle and took a quick
photo of the empty but waiting church, the scent
of lilies and roses filling the air. It was a promise of forever, waiting for the people to arrive and
make it a reality.

"We're going to the back?" Drew asked.

She nodded. "Yes. There's a room there where
the groom should be. If not yet, soon." A few
guests had already arrived but were mingling outside until seating began. "Can you take this stuff
back? I'm going to get a few sanctuary shots while
it's empty."

"No problem, boss." He flashed her a smile and
headed toward the back of the church.

Harper took a moment to stop and absorb the
character of the church. There was a peace here,
and a level of excitement, too, for the joining of
two lives together. Weddings were so optimistic
and happy. Before long the seats would be full, and
the bride would walk up the aisle in her white dress

to meet her husband. They'd make promises. She lifted her camera and looked through the viewfinder. The flowers were so fresh and pretty. She took a photo of the table set up for signing the register, a small plumed pen on top of the linen along with a spray of more flowers. Finally, she turned around at the front of the altar and looked back toward the closed door of the sanctuary. Strong and sturdy, the wood was dark with age and she wondered how many brides had crossed its threshold.

And she took a photo of that, too.

Then she made her way to where the groomsmen—and Drew—waited.

CHAPTER TWELVE

COMING WITH HARPER today had been a mistake.

He'd wanted to spend the day with her and he'd wanted to help since Juny wasn't available. But he'd miscalculated. Being at a wedding with Harper was another thing entirely. All around him were reminders of how the world generally worked. You grew up, fell in love, got married, settled down. Locked in.

The ceremony itself had been intimate and warm, with smiles abounding. He'd watched Harper scoot around the church, taking pictures without ever being in the way, admiring her for that talent alone. He'd stood by her side and endured the after-wedding pictures of the receiving line, and then once again for wedding party and family pictures at the reception venue, a hotel on the outskirts of the town. The relatively small number of guests—under seventy, as close as he could guess—mingled by tents set up outside, sipping glasses of punch and champagne, while Harper took photo after photo of the bride and groom and the special people in their lives.

It made him feel claustrophobic.

"Are you okay?" Harper asked, reaching in her bag for the second camera with a different lens. "It's hot. Is the sun too much?"

"No, of course not. But would you like something to drink? Water?"

"That would be great. The sun is really baking things today."

He escaped to find some water and as a member of the waitstaff poured two glasses for him, he overheard two people talking a few feet away as they sipped pink punch.

"Oh, yes, they've bought a house, only a few blocks from Pat and Susan. Pris is going to substitute teach for now, and Rob's got his job at the insurance company."

Drew dug in his pocket for a tip for the bartender.

"They thought about moving to Calgary, apparently, but she wanted to stay close to her parents."

"It's so good they've both got work. I know Pris doesn't want to wait for a family, either."

Drew's throat tightened and that knot of panic centered in his chest again. This was literally his worst nightmare. Working in insurance? Living two blocks from his in-laws? Tied down with babies?

He grabbed the glasses from the counter and

headed back to where Harper was taking photos of the bride and groom alone now that the family obligations were over. When she finished the current pose, she took a moment to have a drink while the bride stood and fluffed out her dress.

"Oh, that's good. Thank you."

"You're welcome."

Her smile was sweet as she looked into his eyes. "This is the nicest wedding. They're so in love. And that little church…it was perfect. I love intimate weddings like that."

"It's definitely beautiful," he agreed, but his jaw was tight.

"Are you okay?"

He pasted on a smile. "You already asked that, and of course I am. What happens after this?"

She took another drink and handed him the glass. "We'll take a few more of the bride and groom alone, and then the reception is mostly informal. More of a garden party sort of thing, with a few speeches later on." She sighed. "And no dance. The happy couple are leaving on a honeymoon tonight, so they're going home to change and get a ride to the airport."

She put her hand on her belly. "I'm not sorry. It means my day will be over before seven, rather than nine or ten."

He put aside his own discomfort and put his hand on her arm. "Is there anything I can do?"

She shook her head. "No. Give me fifteen minutes and we can get something to eat. Then I'll snap some candids, and ones of the speeches."

"Okay."

He stood back while she went to the couple and they decided on a few more shots with the mountains in the background. He watched as she took a few of the couple walking away, and then one as the groom scooped the bride up in his arms.

He could imagine scooping Harper up like that, and hearing her laugh as she settled in his arms.

Invisible walls began closing in. What was he doing? He shouldn't be here. He should have done what Dan had said and stayed away from her from the beginning. But how could he have known that actual feelings would get in the way? That she'd be different? The trouble was, this was the kind of life Harper wanted. Settled. A routine. Babies. The whole white-picket-fence deal. He'd been able to tell when she'd talked about wanting them someday and the look in her eyes when she'd confessed she thought this might be her only chance. She wanted children and she should have them. God, they had really been fooling themselves, acting like this thing between them didn't matter. That they could come away unscathed.

Finished for the moment, he helped Harper gather the camera bags and they made their way to a small table on the perimeter of the eating area. Harper looked like she'd gotten a bit of sunburn, so he told her to stay at the table and he'd bring back food. He returned with a plate for each of them containing finger sandwiches, scones, little pots of jam, and something called clotted cream.

"I looked for vegetarian options," he explained, putting her plate down. "I found cucumber and watercress and a couple of cheese kinds. And scones, of course."

His own plate contained slightly heartier choices: sliced chicken and salmon, along with the same assortment of scones.

"It's perfect. Just what I need." She let out a sigh of relief, but Drew realized he hadn't brought them drinks.

"Do you want tea? Or sparkling water or something?"

A server passed by with a tray of dirty glasses and overheard. "Can I bring you both a beverage?"

What he really wanted was a beer. Instead, he asked for another glass of champagne, the only alcohol that seemed to be available. Harper asked for sparkling water and then picked up a sandwich.

He ate, too, but didn't really taste the food. He wanted to go, to escape, but also wanted to stay for her. What he really wanted was to be chilling out on her front porch in a pair of jeans, a cold beer and a soft breeze. This wasn't the place for him, for them. He and Harper focused on the moment, not on forever. They weren't dresses and dainty things posing as sandwiches. They were lemonade and lazy naps on a swing and…

Maybe this wasn't really love after all. Maybe he was simply caught up in it, in her. An infatuation. Enjoying playing hooky from work and getting out of the rat race.

Yeah. That had to be it. It was the only thing that made sense.

Harper got up to get dessert, a selection of things she called petit fours and Madeleines…it all sounded French and fancy to him, though they tasted fine.

"You look like you'd rather have a steak than that canapé," Harper said, and he realized he'd been zoned out for a few minutes.

"Yeah. This isn't really my style."

"Weddings come in all shapes and sizes," she responded. "Last year Adele did one that used dog sleds to transport everyone to the ceremony location. Dan and Adele's was at the Cascade, I've done ones in people's living rooms, on riverbanks…and in a kayak." She looked up at him and laughed. "The thing is, everyone has to do what's right for them and what they want. A garden party on the lawn is not my idea of the perfect reception—for me."

She looked out over the assembled group. "This is pretty and all, but I'm lower maintenance than that. I loved the little church today, with close friends and family. Then something informal, like spaghetti and salad around a big table with lots of laughter. I want my wedding to reflect how I want to live my life. Fully."

The noose tightened, because as much as he wanted to run, he also didn't want any other man giving that life to her.

He was saved from answering by the emcee, the best man, standing up to the mic. Harper slipped out of her seat and got her camera ready, moving to the back of the tent for a good vantage point.

He needed to let her go. And didn't want to. But it was for the best.

Harper had no idea what had gotten into Drew today, but he hadn't been himself since the ceremony. The sun was in her eyes as they headed into town, and she put the visor down as she squinted. "Do you want to come over?" she asked quietly.

"I should probably go back to the hotel. I've got a lot of work to do tomorrow."

She glanced over at him. "Tomorrow is Sunday."

He met her gaze briefly and swallowed.

"I don't know what happened today, but something did," she said, her voice a little stronger. "So if you want to go back to the hotel, it's fine."

He sighed. "When a woman says it's fine, I know it's anything but."

She looked over again. "I'm fine, really. But I don't think you are."

And she wasn't really either, but she hadn't withdrawn today as he had. Something was going on in his head. She'd hoped they would end up having a fun day together. After all, weddings were romantic.

Maybe that was the problem. She stared at the road ahead and reminded herself that just because she'd fallen for him didn't mean he felt the same way. She was certain he liked her a lot. And their chemistry was off the charts. But she wasn't totally naive. She knew that chemistry wasn't love.

Instead of turning up the hill to the hotel, she pulled into the parking lot for Bow Falls. There were still a few cars in the parking lot; as long as there was light there'd be a few people looking at the water rushing over the falls, but the crowds of the day had dissipated.

"I don't want to have this talk at the passenger drop-off," she said quietly, killing the engine.

"Harper, I… Dammit. I don't know what to say."

"Maybe you can start with what happened this afternoon. We went to the church and you were fine. Headed to the reception and suddenly you didn't seem to know what to do with yourself. You didn't smile, didn't say much. And I don't know why. Did I do something?"

"No!" He was so fast to respond that she knew he meant it, and she gave a little sigh of relief. He sighed heavily. "I was fine until I went to get the water for us, you know? And I heard a couple of ladies talking, and it made a few things clear for me, that's all."

"Some random women you don't know said something at a wedding and you achieved sudden clarity?" She tried to lighten the mood, but her joke fell flat, instead sounding sarcastic.

He looked over at her. "Harper, we want different things. We know it, and we've chosen to ignore it. But we shouldn't have. You were right at Dan and Adele's wedding. Flings are a mistake."

She tilted her head, examining him. "You know, we talked about all this. You're leaving next week. You have your life and I have mine, and we made any decisions based on that. So what the hell changed?"

He was quiet so long she felt tears prick the back of her eyes. All she'd wanted was to enjoy the week. To spend time with him while she could. To feel cared for and desired. She wasn't sure what changed but it was hard to believe it happened because of two random strangers.

"So what did they say?"

"What?"

"The women. What did they say?"

"Harper…"

"I know you don't want to have this conversation, but I care about you, Drew. And you care about me. I know you do." He had to, because she'd told him things she hadn't told anyone and she couldn't believe that he would be callous after that.

"I do. God, Harper, so much. And that's the problem." He turned and looked at her, his dark eyes tortured. "I can't do this. I can't be with you and be casual about it, and I can't offer you more. I can't do *this*."

She felt as if she'd been slapped. "I never asked you to 'do this.' Whatever 'this' is."

"I know that." His voice raised a bit, and then he let out a huff of air. "I know that. And yeah, we talked about it. But talking and doing are two different things. I'm leaving to go back to California in a few days."

"That hasn't changed."

"Harper."

"I know. I'm putting you on the spot. But I'm feeling…" She struggled to find the right words, and then knew what the sinking feeling in her stomach was. "I'm feeling blindsided all over again. *It's not you, it's me* right? That's what you were going to say? Thanks for the fun but see ya?"

"You knew this was going to happen."

"But not now. Not...yet."

She wouldn't cry. She wouldn't. But she'd felt so alive the past few weeks. He'd made her laugh. Challenged her. Kissed her in the middle of the street and bought her ice cream. She'd seen the pictures he'd taken on top of the mountain. Of her. Almost all of her.

Light began to glimmer, along with a little hope. "Do you love me, Drew?"

His lips dropped open in surprise. "What?"

"Do. You. Love. Me." She said each word deliberately. "Is that what has you running?"

He swallowed, his throat bobbing, while her heart beat crazily in her chest. "No," he whispered, the word filling the car with finality. "And today I realized you will always be the woman who wants to put down roots. To have the place to belong you never had. That's not me, Harper, and I can't lead you on and let you pretend it is. I'm always going to be the one who needs to keep moving. I can't be fenced in."

"Why? What scares you so much?"

He didn't answer, and she knew he wasn't going to, either. It was what it was and nothing she said would change it.

"Those women...the bride wants babies right away. They're buying a house two blocks from her parents and he's working for an insurance company. My God, that's my worst nightmare."

Anger started to seep in past the confusion and hurt. "Did I ever say I wanted any of that?"

"No, but you do want roots. You made that clear. Your life is here. You finally have a home."

"And would living here be so bad? You'd be close to your brother. In the mountains. You'd have a store here."

She took a pause and added, "And I'd be here."

"So you do want it, even if you didn't say it."

"Maybe," she shot back. "But I knew you didn't. So I never brought it up. I feel like you're blaming me for something I didn't even do."

The interior of the car went silent and they both stared out the window. Yes, she'd fallen in love with him, but she'd never made any demands. She'd known better. And instead he'd turned around and ruined what might have been a few wonderful last days together.

That was what she'd wanted. No unrealistic expectations. But a perfect week of happiness. Something to show her she was worth it. Instead she got this. Excuses because he was afraid.

She turned in her seat and looked over at him. For years she'd closed herself off from feeling. Don't get wrapped up in someone and they can't hurt you. She'd done it as a girl with friends. As a teen and then a young woman with relationships— she'd always been the first to leave or break it off so she was in control of the hurting. Jared's abandonment had only confirmed that philosophy.

But that was over. It wasn't living. She'd started to learn with her friendship with Adele, and maybe it was the emotions stirred up by the pregnancy or just her time with Drew, but she wasn't going to close herself off anymore. She was going to feel, dammit.

Feel everything. Even when it hurt.

"If this is it, Drew, then I'm going to be honest with you. I think you're being a coward right now. I think you care and you're running scared. Or maybe to you I'm not worth it. I know how I feel. You told me that I wasn't plain or ordinary. That I was kind and generous. You made me feel like I could finally step out from behind the lens and be me. And you made me fall in love with you. I'm not afraid to say it. I thought I would be, but I'm not anymore." She took a big breath. "I love you, and I never once considered asking you for more because it would mean asking you to stop being you. So don't put this on me, okay? If you want to be done, say so. I never put any pressure on you for more and we both know it."

His jaw tightened and silence dropped like a hammer in the car. She knew he couldn't say those words back. The longer he was silent, the more horrible it became. Finally he was able to form a few words. "I think I should go back to the hotel now. I can walk back if you don't want to drive."

That was it? She said I love you and she got nothing? Worse than nothing. She turned the key in the ignition and the engine came to life. "I'll take you." Inside she was crumbling, but only a little. Not because she was wrong, but because she was sad that this was the way it was ending. He wouldn't even talk.

The drive took about a minute and a half, but it felt much longer as neither of them spoke on the way. She parked in the passenger drop-off and left the engine running, though she put the car in Park.

"Harper... I didn't want it to end like this. I swear I didn't. I thought I could do this week and just walk away. But it's not fair. Not to you, not to me. We were fooling ourselves, you know? I don't want this to end with you angry with me."

She looked over at him, frustrated and sad and disappointed and a lot of other emotions she couldn't sort through yet. "I *am* angry with you, Drew. You were the one who pursued me. Who kissed me. Who made me believe I could step outside myself and take a chance. You whisked me off in a helicopter and took me to dinner and invited me to your hotel room. And now you're the one backing away. I'm disappointed. Not because we're over, because I always knew we would be.

But because you freaked out at a stupid wedding and did it this way."

"I don't want it to be like this. I want us to part with a smile and good wishes. Please, Harper. Understand I'm doing this because I don't want to hurt you."

She felt a trembling start inside and braced herself against it, wanting to be alone when the crying started. "It's too late for that," she answered, staring at a nick on the leather of the steering wheel.

He cursed beneath his breath, then undid his seat belt.

He was leaving. Walking away, just like everyone else. Not the way they'd agreed, but on his terms, because once again she didn't matter. Not enough. Fool me once, shame on you. Fool me twice…love had made a fool of her again. And still, she couldn't bring herself to regret it.

Her breath caught in her chest, strangling her.

He got out, then looked inside at her, his eyes sad and lips drooping. "I'm sorry, Harper, I really never wanted to hurt you. I think this is for the best. Like ripping off a Band-Aid."

For him. And that was fine. She'd relied on herself for a long time, and she'd do so again.

"Goodbye, Drew," she said, a hitch in her voice.

After a long moment, he sighed. "Bye, Harper."

He straightened and shut the door. For one prolonged second, she hesitated, wanting him to open the door and say it was all a mistake. That he loved her, too, that he was sorry for being afraid and a jerk and that he wanted to go home with her and make everything right.

But that wasn't Drew. It never had been, and she knew it, so she resolutely put the car in gear and pulled away.

And she didn't look in the rearview mirror, either.

CHAPTER THIRTEEN

DREW HAD ASKED Dan to drive him to the airport. There was no reason to stay in Banff any longer; any business with the building purchase could easily be handled from Sacramento. He'd been staying mostly to handle things in person and be close to Harper, but now he knew it was time to go.

Dan pulled up to the hotel entrance and got out of his car. "Hey, brother. This is everything?"

He tended to travel light. There was one suitcase, and his backpack that doubled as a carry-on. "This is it. Thanks for the lift." He'd had his rental picked up last night. And he could have hired a car service, but he felt the need to see his brother before leaving again.

"No problem. I'm going into the office a little later, is all."

Drew had found an earlier flight even though it wasn't as convenient a route. The sooner he got back, the better. He could get his life back to normal.

They loaded his bags and then headed toward

Calgary. A light mist was falling, giving the day a grey, dismal feeling. Drew seemed to remember high school English and something about rain and sad bits of stories being pathetic fallacy. Whatever. She'd called him a coward and maybe she was right. But mostly he figured she represented everything he didn't want for himself. This was for the best.

Except he couldn't stop thinking of the words she'd said. *I love you* had come out of her lips and had rattled him right to his shoes. Because being with her was the closest he'd ever come to uttering those same words.

I love you didn't mean enjoying each other for two weeks. It meant a much bigger investment and much bigger stakes. And for all his success, Drew knew one thing. He took only calculated risks. This one had volatility written all over it.

"You're awfully quiet."

"Just thinking of everything I have to do when I get back."

"Hmm."

"Hmm?" Drew looked over at his brother.

"What happened between you and Harper? Because something did, didn't it?"

Irritation flared, and Drew's lips thinned. "So what if it did? Harper's her own woman."

Dan's brows knit together. "She is, and that's

your way of telling me to mind my own business. Except Harper is my business, in a way."

"No, she's not." Drew remembered all of Harper's frustrated sighs and irritation blossomed into indignation. "You might have a baby in her belly, but she's not yours to command, brother."

Dan's lips dropped open. "Holy hell. Where did that come from? Did I say I wanted to 'command' her? And there's no need to be so crude. She's our surrogate. It's not like I slept with her, for God's sake."

Drew tried to get a rein on his temper. Only part of it was Dan; he was also mad at himself for being an idiot. For starting something in the first place. He'd been a fool, thinking he could do something like that and come away unscathed. Because even though leaving was the only solution, he still knew he'd hurt her, and that had been the last thing he wanted. This was exactly why he didn't do relationships.

When Drew didn't answer, Dan let out a slow breath. "Harper is Adele's best friend. So yeah, I'm a bit protective."

"Oh, come on, Dan. You weren't anything like this at the wedding and I made no secret of flirting. The difference now is that she's carrying a baby for you and somehow that means you and Adele have felt like you have a say in everything she does."

"If you mean I didn't want her to get hurt when

you left, you're right. We all knew you'd be picking up and leaving again, whenever the fancy struck you."

That stung. It made him sound unreliable, which he wasn't.

"It's more than having to do with me." He tightened his fingers into fists, trying to measure his words better. "All of a sudden you guys were watching what she ate and where she went and if she was okay going on a hike she's done a zillion times. For God's sake, do you think she'd be careless or take unnecessary chances? But all you guys do is hover. And I know this is important to you. This is your baby and a bit of a miracle. Harper gets that, too. But I've watched you guys over the last few weeks. You treat her like you don't trust her, or you act like she isn't even there."

Dan's face was blanked with surprise. "That's not true."

"She's carrying this baby, Dan. It's part of her. She gets attached, too, you know. All this is happening to her, but sometimes you leave her out of the equation. She told me about the day you heard the heartbeat. She was really moved by it, and you and Adele acted as if she wasn't even there. Like the sum total of her purpose was her uterus. And she's more than that. So very much more."

She was everything. He swallowed thickly.

Silence overtook the vehicle, and Drew wondered if he'd pushed his brother too far. When he finally chanced a look over at Dan's profile, he saw his brother's throat bobbing as if he was trying to swallow a lump the size of an egg.

"We got too caught up in ourselves," Dan finally whispered.

"Well, do better. She's given up a lot to give you this gift, and I know the baby is important, but you guys seem to have forgotten all the other good things about her. Do you ever talk about anything other than the baby when you're together?"

Dan's cheeks coloured. He looked over at Drew. "Are you in love with her?"

It was Drew's turn to swallow. "No," he lied softly. "And even if I was, she needs someone better than me. She wants a home and stability and someone like you, Dan. Who'll be willing to stay in one place and settle down. That's not me. It wouldn't work and we'd only end up hurting each other."

More silence, and then Dan spoke up. "You know, at one point Adele and I nearly didn't get back together. It wasn't until I realized that I would do anything to see her happy that it all came together. You're putting her feelings first, Drew. That sounds like love to me."

Drew scoffed, hoping his big brother was wrong. "After a few weeks? Please. Anyway, I've got to get back to run my business. Plus I have a trip booked at the end of August. There's a lot to do between now and then. I can't lounge around a resort town indefinitely."

He knew he sounded churlish, but he couldn't help it. He believed only about half of what he was saying and he was pretty sure Dan wasn't buying it all, either. But it didn't matter. He was getting on that plane today and they would all get back to normal.

Except he couldn't forget how she'd looked the night before last when she'd dropped him off at the hotel.

I love you, and I never once considered asking you for more because it would mean asking you to stop being you. So don't put this on me, okay? If you want to be done, just say so. I never put any pressure on you for more and we both know it.

He did know it. And it was why he felt so crappy. She'd accepted him as he was, without reservation, even after all her hurts and insecurities.

And he'd done nothing but blame her for hers.

She was better off without him.

January

When the pains started, Harper was at the studio, editing Juny's photos from a New Year's wedding.

When her water broke, she was back at home, thinking the contractions had been more Braxton Hicks, and she'd made herself a bowl of vegetable soup and a grilled cheese sandwich for supper. The moment it happened she'd had a fleeting bit of panic, and then she'd picked up the phone, called Dan and Adele, and prepared for the trip to the hospital. The wait was nearly over, and soon she would have the baby and put her in Adele's arms and go back to her previously scheduled life.

For a moment, emotion washed over her and she wanted to cling to these last moments, despite the pain, despite the discomfort of the last few weeks of pregnancy, despite everything. She and this baby had made a nine-month journey together. It was nearly over and to her surprise, she wasn't quite ready. She ran her hand over her engorged stomach, memorizing the hardness, closing her eyes and imprinting this moment to keep close to her heart for always. "I love you, little one," she whispered. "You're gonna see your mama and daddy soon. But I'm always going to be here for you, you'll see."

And then her body took over and she couldn't think of anything except breathing through the contractions as she waited for Dan and Adele to arrive.

The drive to the hospital was a blur, though she felt a moment of thanks when she realized the flurries of earlier had stopped and the roads were clear. Dan drove and Adele sat in the back with her, holding her hand, watching her closely and timing contractions. When a pain hit, they breathed together, and Harper felt tears burn her eyelids.

This was such a huge moment. She'd wanted to do this for her friends so badly, but she'd grossly underestimated how difficult it would be to separate herself from the baby that wasn't hers. In the end, Dan and Adele would go home, a complete little family, and she'd be alone…again.

"You hang in there," Adele soothed, rubbing Harper's hand. "I'm here. You squeeze as hard as you need."

Harper gasped and laughed. "I'll break your fingers. Just keep talking to me. It helps."

"You bet." Adele let out a long breath, and Harper followed her lead. She looked up as the contraction waned and Adele cleared her throat. "Harper…" Her voice was thick. "I know things got a little weird in the beginning, and it seemed I thought more about the baby than I did about you." When Harper started to protest, Adele shook her head. "No, don't say it's not true. Drew said as much to Dan at the time, and brought us to our senses."

At the mention of Drew's name, a familiar pain shot to her chest. She pushed it aside.

"We were insensitive, you know? And excited and scared and overwhelmed. But you… Harper, you're our miracle. You're a part of our family, and you always will be."

Harper sniffled a little and squeezed Adele's hand, gently. "And you're my family, too," she whispered. "The kind you choose, you know? Besides, I forgot all about that months ago. Going through this with you…it's been a blessing and a privilege."

There wasn't much time to talk about it more as another contraction hit, faster than before. They got to the hospital and were taken straight to a room. Nurses bustled in and got her into a gown, hooked up a fetal monitor and checked her progress. With her pains only four minutes apart, things were moving along so quickly she could barely catch her breath.

"You had pains all day, didn't you?" the kind nurse said, reading the results of the monitor.

"They started this morning. I thought they were more Braxton Hicks."

"You should have called!" Adele chided, sitting on the side of the bed and tucking a stray piece of hair behind Harper's ear. Dan stood behind, looking slightly out of place. But Harper knew he wanted to be here and so she sent him a smile.

"You spent most of the day in first stage, I think," the nurse said. "The good news is, it won't be long now."

And it wasn't. Less than an hour later, Isabelle Janice Brimicombe came screaming into the world, much to the delight of her mother and father and Harper.

"We want you to be her godmother," Adele said, once the room had quieted and the three of them were left alone for a few minutes. Adele held the baby in her arms, and Harper felt a rush of emotion she couldn't quite define. Happiness and sadness and fullness and emptiness all at once, but she knew that no matter what, she'd be there for Isabelle, and answering yes was the easiest thing in the world.

"We can never repay you for the gift you've given us," Dan said, his hand on Adele's shoulder. Tears glimmered in his eyes. "Harper, I…" Overcome with emotion, he laughed a little as tears slid down his cheeks. "I have a daughter because of you. *Thank you* hardly seems like anything."

Of course she was happy for them. This was what she'd wanted for Adele. Now Harper had roots in this town because of their relationship. It was her home. There was nothing more important.

Adele handed the baby to Dan and took Harper's hands in hers. "I want you to know," she said quietly, tears clogging her voice, "that you are the sister I never had and always wanted. I love you, Harper. Dan's right. I can never repay you for what you've given us."

She sniffed, emotion getting the better of her. "I feel the same, sweetie. Besides, no repayment is necessary." She gave them a tired smile. "Now, as much as I love you guys, the nurse is going to come back in a few moments, and I'm going to have a shower and put on some pajamas. I'm not sure I need spectators for that." She looked up at Dan, who was staring at Isabelle's face with such awe her heart melted. "The baby will spend the night in the nursery and we'll all go home tomorrow, right?"

Adele nodded. "Yes. Oh my gosh, yes. Home."

The nurse came in with a smile. "Okay, happy family. It's time to get Harper fixed up. You feeling a bit wobbly, hon?"

She nodded. "A little, but I think I'll be fine."

Once Dan, Adele and the baby were ushered away, the nurse gently helped Harper out of bed and to the bathroom and shower. "Take your time," she said, "and go ahead and sit down if you need to. The warm water is going to feel great, and before you know it we'll have you in a comfy bed for a well-deserved sleep."

The shower was already running and Harper stepped inside, holding on to a bar for stability. She felt fine, really. At least physically. Now that the pains were over, she was tired. And the nurse was right. The hot water felt heavenly.

But as she stood under the spray, tears came to her eyes and slipped down her cheeks. Her breath came in sharp gasps and she tried to be quiet so she didn't alarm the nurse, who she knew would be somewhere nearby. But she couldn't help it, couldn't explain it. She cried…for the baby she'd carried, for the baby who was now someone else's, for the one she would probably never have, for the life she was now going to have to go back to, empty and lonely.

And when she had cried herself out, she shut off the shower, and the nurse silently helped her dry and get dressed, not commenting on Harper's blotchy face. Instead she retrieved a tissue for Harper to blow her nose, and got her settled in a wheelchair to take her to a private postnatal room.

The baby was healthy and now it was time for Harper to reset—physically, mentally and emotionally. It was time for her to get back to her own life.

And yet somehow she got the feeling nothing was going to be quite the same.

She was home by three the next afternoon, sitting in the back of Dan's car along with the car seat and a sleeping Isabelle inside. She reached out and touched her finger to the soft blanket keeping the baby warm, her little eyelids nearly translucent beneath the pink knitted cap. At home, Adele offered to help her inside, but Harper smiled and shook her head. "Go home with Dan and Isabelle," she said softly. "I'm going to make some tea, grab a book and rest for a while."

And so Adele and her little family left her just inside her doorway.

Life would return to normal now, she thought. Except it couldn't, because too much had happened for it to look like it had only ten months earlier, before she'd started going to the doctor appointments, before the pregnancy test. She was different now; she could feel it deep inside, like somehow her DNA had changed.

She took exactly two days off work. On the third day she was back at the studio, working at her computer. Not pushing herself, but she needed to get back into a regular routine. She edited and put together packages for clients. Went back to earlier in the summer and pulled up wildlife photos and landscapes, scouring them for ones worthy of showing out front. She came in one day and discovered that her mama and babies grizzly print had sold, but Juny said it was an off-the-street purchase. The sales receipt showed a name and address from Calgary. She was sad to see it go.

She replaced it with the grizzly photo from Stewart Canyon, but in doing so, she went through the photos of the day and caught the ones of Drew and the bighorn sheep. She stared at them for long minutes, wondering what in the world was wrong with her. She was going through the motions. Nothing excited her. The photos of Drew made her sad. She worked each day and then went home and stared at the TV, or went to bed since she always seemed tired. It was like living life in black and white after being in bright, wonderful colour.

She lost her baby weight.

Aspen Outfitters announced a grand opening of the second week of February, right around Valentine's Day, when Isabelle would be a month old. The store sign was installed and Opening Soon banners placed in the windows. Now Harper had a reminder of Drew whenever she walked down Banff Avenue to some of her favorite haunts. She couldn't look at Cow's Ice Cream the same, either.

When Drew left she'd had the pregnancy to keep her going. Now she felt as if she had nothing. Work wasn't the same. She couldn't get up any enthusiasm for their scheduled photo shoots. It seemed as if she was photographing the same things over and over. Home wasn't the same, either. All she'd wanted as long as she could remember was a home of her own. Now she had it…and it wasn't enough.

She'd always heard the saying be careful what you wish for. Now she knew what it meant. If the life she'd created for herself wasn't the answer to her loneliness, what was?

CHAPTER FOURTEEN

DREW HUDDLED INSIDE his coat against the freezing rain that was falling. In just over a week the Banff location was going to open, and the hectic but brilliant finishing touches were under way before the grand opening. Another store would open in Whistler in the summer. He should be happy. Canadian expansion was happening, the business was growing, and he'd had a fantastic trip to Switzerland in September. Life was exactly as he wanted it.

Except he was unhappy, and angry at himself for it.

He jogged to his truck. By the time he got it unlocked and inside, his hair was wet with icy droplets.

He drove by Harper's studio on his way back to the hotel. He'd missed her more than he cared to admit. Nothing had been the same since the summer. For God's sake, he'd gone out on two dates and had found himself comparing the women—unfavorably—with Harper within ten minutes.

Being in Banff only made it worse. Dan was a

new dad, proud as anything of his baby daughter, sleep-deprived and blissfully happy. Even looking at the baby reminded Drew of Harper. He remembered the awe on her face when he'd put his hand on her belly after hearing the heartbeat, or the way she'd fallen asleep on the porch swing, peaceful and so very beautiful.

He'd get over her eventually, and it would be easier. Right?

Except he couldn't stop thinking about her. Last night Dan had taken him aside and mentioned how he and Adele were worried about her. "Adele and I think she's feeling very alone right now. You might have broken her heart, Drew, and now she doesn't have the pregnancy to keep her going. Adele lets her spend lots of time with the baby, and she seems happy, but…"

Drew turned down her street and parked a few houses away from hers. He rested his head on the steering wheel. The idea of actually breaking Harper's heart caused him real physical pain. As much as he didn't want to admit it, nothing had been right since he'd gone home at the first of August. He'd left a piece of himself back in Banff. He had fallen in love with Harper despite his best efforts not to.

And now he had to make a choice. Either keep his distance, or take the few steps to her door and see her once more.

He shut off the engine and let out a sigh. He remembered her saying she was worried about being attached to the baby, about getting too close. If nothing else, he could be a friend and make sure she was okay.

The knock on the door was unexpected. It was past six and neither Adele nor Dan had called to say they were coming over. With the new baby, surprise drop-ins didn't happen as often as they used to.

Juny and Adele and Dan had all expressed concern over her, and she kept answering that she was just bouncing back and a little tired. It was much easier than coming out with the complicated truth—that she was dissatisfied with the life she'd thought she wanted.

Or that she'd let Drew in and got her heart broken. That was a big part of it, even if she wouldn't admit it out loud to a single soul.

She looked through the peephole and her breath seemed to strangle in her throat. Drew, looking handsome as ever, stood in the glow of her porch light in a down jacket, his breath making frosty clouds in the air.

Drew. Out of thin air.

Hands shaking, she unlocked the door and opened it. "Hi," she said, standing back.

"Hi. Can I come in?"

"Too cold to stay out there."

He stepped inside, his gaze sweeping her from head to toe and back up again. "Dan was right," he said, his voice low. "You look awful."

The words were a gut punch but also fired some indignation. "Gee, thanks. Is that all you came to say? I mean, it's a Friday night, I'm off work and I'm allowed to lie around in sweats and a hoodie if I want to."

"Sorry," he answered, and unzipped his coat. Apparently he was planning to stay. She could ask him to leave, but while he'd opened with a negative comment, she was still so glad to see him that she couldn't bear to send him away so soon.

She figured she shouldn't. The truth was she still loved him.

Then it occurred to her what he'd said. "Dan called you?"

He nodded. "Not a call, per se. I'm in town to oversee the opening next week. He might have said something last night after dinner."

All of her feelings bubbled up into her chest and throat, but she didn't say them. Instead she said, "I'm fine. I'm back at work and taking some downtime when I'm not shooting or at the studio. That's it." She did have some pride, after all. Before he'd gone back to California, she'd opened her heart to him. He'd rejected it. It wasn't likely she'd do the same thing again in a hurry.

Even if it was true.

"Dan seemed to think you were feeling down."
He hung his jacket over a kitchen chair, looked at
her for a minute and then sighed. "Harper, I remember how you were starting to have feelings
about the pregnancy. Feeling attached to the baby.
You went through all that and it's not surprising
that you might be lonely now that it's over. Or…
sad." He'd done a bit of googling again. "Like…
maybe postpartum depression or something."

Postpartum depression? She gawped at him for
a full ten seconds, unable to respond. She had no
doubt such a thing was possible; she'd done a fair
bit of research herself. But that wasn't what was
going on with her. Her dissatisfaction came from
wanting more. Because he'd shown her that life
could be an adventure and she wanted more of it.

"I'm not depressed," she said firmly. "But you're
right. Something changed. And I'm not quite sure
what to do about it yet."

"I don't understand."

He looked genuinely perplexed. She went to the
cupboard and took out a glass, filled it with water
and handed it to him. "Here. Have a drink and sit
down."

He did, and she sat in the chair closest to him,
with just the corner of the table between them.
He took a drink and put down the glass. "What
changed? Does it have to do with Isabelle?"

"No, not really." She thought about the little girl and couldn't help the smile that spread across her lips. "She's adorable. And when I see Dan and Adele…it was the right thing, Drew. They're so happy. I'll always have a special bond with Belle. How could I not? But I have no regrets."

He nodded, his eyes sober. "I'm glad. I was worried about that…"

The irritation flared again. "Why would you worry? You left. I haven't heard from you since the summer, even though I know you've been in town. I don't need you to check up on me, Drew. I'm doing just fine."

His jaw hardened. "If that's so, why are Dan and Adele worried about you?"

She tried to sound strong. And she was, really. But this was hard. There were times over the past five months that memories of Drew had kept her going. The times they'd shared had been magical.

He leaned forward. "It's okay to not be strong all the time. I know how much you want a family of your own, and how having the baby must have—"

She pushed away from the table, cutting him off. "You really think this has to do with the baby? I'm proud of what I did. I'm so incredibly happy for Adele and Dan, and yeah, it had its moments but I'd do it all over again. If I'm unhappy, Drew, it's not because of sweet Isabelle. It's because I have a home and a family here, and my own business, and it's no longer enough. And you did that. You took me on adventures and made me want more out of my life. That's my problem. I'm not happy with the life I thought I always wanted."

She met his gaze. "Last summer, I told you I loved you and you ran. That's on you, Drew. And yeah, maybe I wanted to finally have some stability. But you know what? I wasn't running scared." She lifted her chin. "And I'm still not."

He looked so shocked that she softened her voice. "But you still are. I'm not a fragile flower, Drew. But I have changed. And I'm trying to sort out what I'm going to do about it."

"I…" His gaze slid away from her, and then back again. "I didn't know, Harper."

She exhaled through her nose, tried to calm her beating heart. "I know. And yes, you were there for me last summer. Getting over you hasn't been easy, okay?" Seeing him again was going to set her back a few steps, too. "You should probably go."

He got up from his chair and went to her. "Not like this. Not angry. We left last time with you being angry, and I don't like it."

"Why is that, do you think?" She tried to ignore the touch of his warm hands as he reached out for her fingers.

"Because people don't generally say no to me?"

She couldn't help the surprised smile at his honesty and insight. "Bingo. But you can't fix this with your charm."

"Nothing's changed for me, really," he said. "I still…"

But he didn't finish. He didn't need to. She knew he wasn't the staying kind, and she also knew she couldn't force someone to be who they weren't.

"You're really okay?" he asked.

"I will be. I just have a lot of things to figure out. I'm not happy, Drew. But no one can fix that but me. I certainly can't rely on anyone else to fix it for me."

She took her hands away from his. "And you. You're opening up the store next week and Adele says another in the summer in British Columbia. You're getting what you wanted."

"Yeah, I guess I am."

Funny, he didn't seem overly excited about it.

"Well, that's good, then." She smiled. He needed to go. She hadn't lied to him but she certainly hadn't been 100 percent truthful. She still had her broken heart to worry about.

"I'd better go. I'm having dinner with Dan and Adele."

"Yes, go. You won't want to be late."

She walked him to the door and held it open as he shrugged on his jacket. He was outside when he turned back and met her gaze.

"Will you come to the opening next week?"

"Yeah, but what if there wasn't a compromise? Because people make ultimatums, too, Dan. I love Mom. She's an amazing woman. But it's always bugged me that she might have held him back from something really great."

"And you don't want that to happen to you."

He let out a relieved breath. "Yes. You get it."

But Dan shook his head. "Sorry, but I don't. It means you're holding your heart back either out of fear or selfishness, and that's not right. Hey, if you're happy being alone, fine. But if you're not, then stop sabotaging good relationships."

Was that what he was doing? Maybe. He certainly wasn't happy. He had been, until…

Until Harper came along and changed everything. Not because he was rich. And his charm didn't work on her, either. She saw past all that and she…

She loved him anyway. She'd loved him even when she had always known he would walk out.

Damn.

"I don't know if I can do it," he murmured, cradling his cup. He looked up at Dan. "I don't know if I have what it takes. I'm not brave like her. Hell, like you." A sideways smile touched his mouth.

Dan laughed. "I'm not brave. Know what it is? It's realizing that life with someone is far less scary than facing life without them. You guys changed each other, and that's pretty amazing. Don't throw it away because of an argument you heard twenty years ago."

When Dan put it like that…

"Better yet," Dan continued, "call Dad and ask him about it. Dad gives good advice."

Drew pulled in a long breath, pursed his lips and let it out slowly, fighting against the wash of emotion. "Yeah," he whispered, suddenly homesick. "He does."

Drew left a little while longer, and once in his hotel room, called his dad. It was late in Ontario, but as always, his parents were ready to chat whenever one of their kids needed them.

"Hey, Dad. I won't keep you long. I just want to ask you a question."

"Sure. Let me go downstairs so I don't keep up your mother."

It took a few moments, then he heard his dad sigh as he sat down in his chair. "What's up?"

"Do you remember, when I was seven or eight, that you had a job opportunity up north?"

"Goodness. Yeah, but that was a long time ago. What about it?"

"Why didn't you take it?"

"Your mother and I didn't want to have to sell the house and move you kids so far. This is a nice neighbourhood. Your friends were here. You were doing well."

Drew stared at the ceiling of his hotel room. "You and Mom decided? Or just Mom?"

He could almost see the wrinkles in his dad's forehead as he answered. "What do you mean?"

"I mean I heard you arguing about it. I know it was a big opportunity for you and she was the one who didn't want to go. And I remember hearing you making comments now and again about being stuck. I guess… I'm wondering if you still resent that. If you wish it had gone differently."

There was a deep sigh. "Drew, sometimes a man weighs what he wants against the needs of his family, and when you love your family, it's no contest. Family comes first."

"Even to sacrifice your own happiness?"

"Is this a choice you're thinking of making, son?"

Drew covered his eyes with his hand. "I don't know. I love her, Dad. But she wants things… things that I think would make me unhappy. How is that good for a marriage?"

"It's not. But there are compromises, Drew. And when it becomes a choice between keeping or losing the person you love…"

"That's what Dan said."

A warm chuckle came across the line.

"I'll be honest, Drew. Marriage is hard sometimes. It takes work. Sometimes we say things we shouldn't. Sometimes we—and by this I mean I—make passive-aggressive comments about things like lost opportunities. But truthfully, the best opportunity in my life was marrying your mother and raising you kids. I would have been a fool to walk away from it."

"But what if…what if I'm not a good…" He struggled over the word, then forced himself to say it. "A good husband. Or father. Am I too selfish for that? I'm so afraid of messing it up."

"We're all afraid of messing it up. It's an important decision. If you *weren't* afraid, then I'd be worried."

A lump formed in Drew's throat. "Thanks, Dad."

"You're welcome. Settling down isn't a sentence, Drew. It's an adventure. Believe me."

Drew laughed, and after a few minutes more they hung up. He stared at the ceiling again, wondering what he was going to do.

And wondering if anything he said would change Harper's mind.

CHAPTER FIFTEEN

DREW WENT TO Harper's house the next night, feeling slightly sick to his stomach from nerves, but knowing he had to see her and try to make things right.

When she opened the door, he caught his breath. There were no sweatpants in sight tonight. Perhaps she'd just got home from work, because she wore a black-and-white dress and heels, while her hair was up in a tidy topknot.

"Drew," she said softly, but she didn't smile. He missed her smile. Wanted to see it on her lips again.

"You look amazing."

"I had a client meeting at six." She stepped aside. "I'm assuming you want to come in."

He nodded. "Yeah. There were things I left unsaid the other night. Things I didn't realize I wanted to say, you know?"

She kept her chin up, but he saw the flash of vulnerability in her eyes and it both tugged at his heart and gave him a sliver of hope.

"Do you want something to drink?" she asked politely.

"No, thank you." When she would have passed by him, he reached out and grabbed her hand, stopping her progress. "Harper. You said the other night that nothing felt right anymore. That you're dissatisfied and want more. And I'm here to say me, too. It's all been wrong since I left, and I'm here to ask if you will give us another chance."

Wide eyes met his. "What changed? Because the other night you were the same Drew as I remember. Scared to death of settling down and leading a dull life."

He huffed out a laugh. "Oh, Harper. Life with you is never boring. I've been an idiot. Blind, stubborn, scared…but the truth is, I love you. I fell in love with you last summer and it scared the hell out of me. But leaving didn't make the feeling go away. It just made me miserable and took all the pleasure out of the life I used to have. I need you, sweetheart. And I'm still scared but I'm done with running."

He let go of her hand and opened his arms. "And I hope if you do any running, it's to right here. Because I'm not sure I can go on living this way."

Without saying a word, she walked into his embrace, and the moment his arms closed around her, she started to cry. He never moved; he let her cry it out, her hands clinging to his shoulders, his fingers stroking along her hair as he sent up a prayer of gratitude.

* * *

Harper breathed deeply and inhaled the scent that was just Drew. He didn't try to shush her, or tell her it was going to be okay. He simply let her be… just as he had last summer when they'd been together. It was one of the things she'd loved about him most. He'd never asked her to be someone she wasn't, and even though he'd walked away, he'd never once expected her to change.

And so she cried, for the heart that had been broken and the emptiness she'd felt in his absence. And when she started to run out of tears, he squeezed her close and kissed the top of her head. "Better?" he asked.

She nodded. "I'm sorry… I shouldn't have bawled all over you."

"It's okay. I'm glad." He stood back and held her upper arms. "I was so afraid you'd turn me away. That I'd messed it up for good."

She shook her head. "I tried to think like you. That maybe no ties, no commitments was the way to go to avoid being hurt. But it didn't work. I couldn't seem to find any joy anymore."

His dark eyes deepened and he took a shaky breath. "It's no guarantee against being hurt. I should know." And his bottom lip wobbled a little bit.

"How do you know?"

He pulled out a kitchen chair and nudged her into

it, and then pulled out another and sat knee to knee with her. He took her fingers in his, an anchor in a swirl of emotional chaos. "I know, Harper, because nothing has been the same since I left here. The business is flourishing and I find I don't have the same excitement or passion anymore. It's like there's a puzzle piece missing, and that piece is you. That day at the wedding, I did freak out. I could see this settled and boring life ahead of me if I gave in to my feelings for you. I knew you wanted to put down roots and I couldn't breathe. I was afraid, so I ran, telling both of us it was for the best."

"So you said," she replied.

"Here's the thing. When I was about eight, I overheard my mom and dad having a fight. Dad was always the stable one, you know? Provider for the family. We grew up in the same house our entire lives. And I thought it was great, until I heard that fight. Until I realized how much my father had given up over the years. Opportunities, promotions that would have involved moving...but Mom never wanted to. She didn't want to make us move schools. Didn't want to leave our neighbourhood. And my dad had another opportunity come up and she didn't want to go and he told her he felt stuck in his life. That she and the kids had held him back from reaching his potential."

"Oh, Drew. That must have made you feel horrible."

"I was eight. I felt at least part of my dad's unhappiness was my fault. And I knew, too, that I didn't want to ever be like that. Caught in a rut and unable to get out, resentful of how my life had turned out. I wanted to set my own terms and travel and not be tied down with a wife and kids who I thought would drain me of my energy and passion."

Harper reached out and took his hand. "We really are two sides of the same coin. My mom and dad loved to move around. It was all about the next adventure. But me... I wanted to stay in one place. Make friends for longer than a year or two at a time. Sleep in the same bedroom and live somewhere long enough that I might actually get tired of the paint and want to redecorate it."

His fingers played with hers as her throat tightened painfully. "The truth is..." She met his gaze evenly, and her lip trembled again. "I think I had all these plans to get back to my regular life after Belle was born, and now I am, and I'm not happy anymore. I'm so scared, Drew. If this is all there is, what's to become of me? I wanted roots. My own house. A business. Friends. It was enough. But it's not anymore."

"And you feel empty."

"Yes!" She was so relieved he seemed to understand.

"Me, too," he said. "I called my dad to ask him about that fight. He remembered it, you know. The company had wanted him to transfer up north. It would have meant a big raise. I asked him if he still resented it and if it had always affected their marriage. And you know what he said?"

She shook her head.

"They made that decision together." He let out a breath and shook his head, as if disbelieving. "Oh, there were still times of stress. Dad wasn't always happy at work and it bled over into his home life. But he told me he had no regrets. Now all this time I let that colour who I was and what I wanted. I wasted so much time on something that wasn't even real. I love my life, I do. But since July... I want something more. I need it. Because nothing's been the same for me either, Harper, and I think that's because I fell in love with you, too." He lifted his hand and placed it on the side of her face. "I don't know how we're going to make it work—or if you even want to. But I really, really want to try."

Something that had been missing for months suddenly flickered to life, right in the center of her chest. It was hope...hope at happiness, hope at love, hope at a future she'd given up on.

She was so overwhelmed. But she clasped his hands and bit down on her lip before saying, "I'd like that. A lot."

"Good." He leaned forward and kissed her forehead. "It's gonna be okay now, all right? We're going to figure it out. Together."

She nodded, and then surprised them both by asking, "Can we get something to eat? For the first time in almost a month, I'm actually starving."

His grin lit up the room. "Yes. Whatever you want. We can hit the town and buy lobster and champagne. We can make a grilled cheese sandwich. As long as I'm with you, I don't care what we eat."

"Pizza. I'd kill for one."

Before she could get up and reach for the takeout menus, though, he touched her knee. "I have one more question to ask, Harper. Will you go to the store opening with me on Thursday?"

A little fizz of excitement ran through her veins. "I'd love to. I can't wait to see what you've done with the place."

"That sounds perfect," he answered, and he leaned forward and finally kissed her. Tears burned in her eyes at the sweetness of it, a depth of emotion that was unexpected. It was a hello. It was a confession. And it was a promise to face things together.

Drew didn't think he'd ever been prouder of a store opening. The shelves and racks were stocked, the new manager was circulating and staff was assisting the invited guests and VIPs who'd come in since the doors opened. A bar was set up in a corner and a caterer had hot finger foods that filled the air with rich, savory scents. It looked magnificent, all polished logs and shiny new fixtures and beautiful displays. Harper was beside him in a long skirt and tall brown boots, her hair done in long curls for the occasion, and a bracelet Drew had given her as a gift at her wrist. Dan and Adele were behind them, with little Isabelle in her mother's arms. His family and the woman he loved… his heart was full. Almost.

There was something that he wanted Harper to see, and he'd had his assistant pull a few strings to make it all come together.

He took Harper by the hand and led her to the huge stone fireplace. Display racks and shelving were designed around it, holding an assortment of upscale backpacking supplies. And above the mantel…

He knew when she noticed because she stopped moving and gasped.

"It was you!" she exclaimed, and he turned around. Her eyes shone at him. "The mama bear and cubs. But Juny said it was a guy from Calgary. And beside it…oh, Drew. I love this shot."

The one she'd taken of the grizzly at Lake Minnewanka hung beside the mama and cubs. Beneath was a gold plaque with her name and studio on it.

"You are so talented, Harper." He tugged her close and put his arm around her. "I got one of the management team to buy the print so you wouldn't know it was me. I thought you hated my guts. And last night Juny opened up and sold my assistant the other. I had someone here to hang it at seven this morning. Happy?"

"Thrilled!"

"I know we haven't made any firm plans, but I don't want you to stop doing this. We can make it happen together. Maybe use Banff and your house here as a home base. We can travel and you can take all the pictures you want, on every continent. Juny can manage things here when you're away."

Adele piped up. "You already said she took over in the last few months you were pregnant, Harper. Gosh, it sounds so exciting."

"Here's the thing," he said, and he captured her gaze. "I understand your need for home and stability, and I'll do what I can to give that to you. You tell me what you need." He took a breath. "Because none of this works without you." Now he understood what his father had meant. It was a matter of priorities. And Harper came first. Nothing worked anymore without her.

She stood on tiptoe and kissed him. "What I wanted most was a home and a place to belong. I thought that was a house and a town and the same people all the time. But that's not what home is, is it?"

"It's not?"

She shook her head. "That stupid old saying is

true. Home really is where the heart is. And my heart's with you, Drew. That's what's been missing. No matter where we are."

Thank God, he thought.

Adele was sniffing behind them and Dan was grinning from ear to ear. "About time," he said gruffly.

And then Harper reached out and took Isabelle from Adele's arms.

"Oh, my," she said softly, and cuddled the baby close to her neck. She closed her eyes. "What am I going to do if I can't see you every day, huh?"

Drew was damned near crying himself at this point. The scene was so utterly perfect. Why had it taken him so long to figure it out? Now wasn't the time, but when it was right, he'd make sure she had babies of her own to love. Their babies. His sons and daughters.

She opened her eyes and looked up at Drew. "I love you. I never stopped. You're really here to stay?"

"As long as you'll have me."

"Us, too," Dan said. "We're your family. That's what we do."

"Always," Drew assured her, putting his arm around her and holding her and Isabelle close. "A family and a man who loves you desperately. And always will."

If he had anything to say about it.

EPILOGUE

HARPER HAD NEVER seen anything quite like the Thorsmork Valley.

It was cool, and she wore a hat and mittens as well as her jacket and hiking boots as they'd climbed all the way up to Magni and Modi, volcanic craters left behind after 2010's massive eruption.

There were times she'd felt on top of the world in her lifetime, but nothing compared to this.

Drew came up beside her. "Doing okay?"

"Perfect," she replied, catching her breath. "I still can't believe we're here."

The first thing Drew had done when they'd arrived was take her to the famed Blue Lagoon, and they'd spent two days in Reykjavik in luxury, being pampered in a spa and adjusting to the jet lag. This morning, though, they'd stopped at Seljalandsfoss Falls and then on to the volcanic hike. The landscape was different from anything she'd ever seen, majestic and sweeping and so very, very old, like something out of Tolkien or George R. R. Martin's books. She'd stopped often and lifted her camera, in such awe and wonder that she didn't know how she was ever going to process it all.

"I told you I wanted to bring you to Iceland someday. Because neither of us had ever been here. A first for us together, you know?"

She leaned in close to him. "I do know. And it's been more than I ever dreamed possible." In the four months since the store opening, Drew had been true to his word. He'd split his time as much as possible between Sacramento and Banff, and she'd made a few trips south, too. He'd shown her his favorite hikes and spots. But this…this was a big step. Their first expedition together.

And it had been so romantic, right from the beginning. Drew had insisted on deluxe accommodations and amenities. She hadn't ever been treated to such luxury. It wasn't how she wanted to live, but it was darned nice on vacation.

But there was something different about Drew today, and Harper turned to face him. "Are you okay?"

He smiled. "I'm perfect. I think. It'll depend."

"Depend on what?"

He reached into his pocket and dropped to one knee. Ahead of them, the tour guide gave a shout and the rest of their party started to whistle as they clued in to what was happening. Harper's heart skipped a beat as she looked down at Drew, who had pulled a tiny box out of his jacket pocket.

"This is our first trip, and I don't want it to be our last. I want to always be beside you, Harper. I want to love you and be what you need. I want to be your home. I want to explore the world with you, and someday I want to put our little son or daughter in a backpack and go on adventures. If you're up for the adventure, will you marry me?"

There was no other answer she could give than yes. With Drew, she'd learned the meaning of home, and of compromise and of the safety that came from leaning on someone you loved and trusted. "Yes," she said, a laugh of joy bubbling up from her throat. "Yes, I'll marry you. Whenever you say and wherever you want to go."

"We'll make an adventurer out of you yet," he said, sliding the ring over her finger, then standing and pulling her into a bear hug as the tour group cheered loudly.

"You already have," she whispered in his ear, ready to take on whatever came next.

* * * * *

*Look out for the previous story in
the Marrying a Millionaire duet*

Best Man for the Wedding Planner

*And if you enjoyed this story,
check out these other great reads
from Donna Alward*

The Cowboy's Convenient Bride
The Cowboy's Christmas Family
The Cowboy's Homecoming
Hired: The Italian's Bride

All available now!